# *Finding Netherfield*

*Olivia Kane*

 ISBN: 9798704265221



Cover design by: Olga Begak Art
Printed in the United States of America

# *CHAPTER ONE*

"Oh, Bingley, it's beautiful! Such gracious proportions and only two miles from Bath," Caroline Bingley exclaimed.

Charles Bingley stood on the wide marble steps of Carlisle Hall, his hands on his hips while he surveyed its extensive property. He took in the massive stone fountain shooting streams of water skyward, the long rows of formal gardens clipped to sharp perfection, the marble figures of Greek gods poised on pedestals that flanked the gravel paths. He looked back at the manor house; two gracious, symmetrical wings of golden stone stretched out from the domed center hall. Glistening windows evenly spaced across its façade reflected the midday sun and gold-leaf carvings curled around the frame of the front door. Carlisle Hall was magnificent and grand and…

"Too much," Bingley muttered.

"I'm sorry?" Caroline asked, squinting into the sun to read her brother's expression.

"I said it's too much," he repeated, turning his face away and walking swiftly towards their coach, his boots crunching on the sweeping gravel drive. Caroline picked up her skirt with one hand and held her parasol high with the other while she hurried after him. "But the lease is within budget, or else why would we have come?"

she queried, catching up to him and walking swiftly by his side to keep pace.

"Thank you very much," Bingley said politely, tipping his hat to the waiting steward. "I will be in touch if interested."

"Thank you, sir. Good day, sir," the graying steward answered, tipping back his shiny hat.

Caroline clutched her brother's arm as he continued striding toward their coach. "What do you mean it's too much?"

Bingley stopped suddenly and flung his free arm toward the massive columns and large pediment that fronted the stately structure.

"It's too big, too imposing, too much responsibility."

"Too big?" Caroline laughed. Was that all? "I was not aware that there could ever be such a thing. You will not be scrubbing the floors yourself; you do know that?"

He sighed, taking a moment to collect his thoughts, thoughts that were barreling toward him so rapidly he could barely express himself. What could he say to make his sister understand more easily?

"Perhaps I am not explaining myself clearly. The thing is, it doesn't quite have the feel I desire." A trickle of perspiration ran down his face. He fumbled for his handkerchief and blotted it quickly. "This feels too grand."

"But isn't an estate supposed to be grand?" Caroline smiled up at him sweetly, oozing persuasion.

"Yes, yes, you are quite correct," he agreed, biting his lip. He stared off into the distance, agitated. The structure was newly built.

Only a year old but already abandoned by its owners.

The midday sun beat down on the gravel, yet there was not an old shade tree to be found within the perimeter of the grounds. All Bingley could see amidst the blinding sunlight was stone and marble and rigid perfection.

It was too hot.

Too mercenary.

Too heartless.

Caroline was surprised by her brother's anxiety. It had been their late father's desire to purchase a large property and, in so doing, complete the family's ascension to landed gentry. Fate had deprived the late Mr. Bingley of fulfilling that dream. Now it fell to his eldest son to carry out his father's wishes.

Not an altogether unpleasant task, Caroline believed.

She was anxious that they settle soon and reap the benefits of being in society with large holdings. But Bingley's amiable nature was dampened by the afternoon's tour, and she knew her brother better than to push him to the point of argument. Instead, Caroline sought to soothe him in the way she knew best.

"This has upset you," she said. "Tell me why."

He shook his head. "I don't know why, exactly. Except I was hoping this place would be more like Pemberley."

"But isn't Pemberley quite grand itself? Or so I've heard."

A broad smile lit up Bingley's face as memories of Pemberley floated back. "Yes, Darcy's Pemberley is just as grand, but it *feels* different. There are roaring fires, and Mrs. Reynolds is always quick to serve iced buns and hot coffee. At Pemberley there are dogs and old sofas and the hunting is just right. Pemberley feels like a home," he said wistfully.

Caroline smiled softly at her impressionable brother. "My, Pemberley does sound enchanting. But is it for sale?"

Bingley's expression of delight faded. "No."

"For lease?"

"No."

"So not an option."

"No." Bingley sighed.

"I see. But can we not have dogs and old sofas and iced buns here as well?"

"Yes, I suppose we could," he said unconvincingly.

"A place like Pemberley is the work of generations. It's likely that any prospective home you tour will feel foreign at first. Indeed, there must have been a moment in time when Pemberley stood just as naked and new under the beating sun," she argued.

He stood there, considering. He felt another trickle of perspiration drip into his eyes, and he blotted it away with his kerchief. His face took on a determined expression.

"No," he said, shaking his head decidedly. "No. There are no shade trees here. I must have shade trees."

The visit was over.

Bingley motioned to the driver to open the door. The driver hopped to attention, and Bingley indicated to Caroline that she should ascend.

"Let's go. I'm unbearably warm," he said with just a hint of impatience.

Caroline hesitated, debating whether or not to continue to press her case or give in with the hope of future victory. She desperately wanted to possess an estate as modern as the one before her and imagined the pleasure she would derive from calling it home.

But, for now, she was at the mercy of Bingley's whims.

She had every confidence in her ability to direct her brother to a fitting property. She very much desired to be an equal partner in the choice as she would share in managing the home. However, their search for an estate was in its infancy; there was nothing to be gained by snapping up the first place they toured.

She sighed slightly and leaning on Bingley's hand for assistance, climbed into the coach.

Five minutes into the drive, she had a new idea.

In a motherly tone, she addressed her brother. "Charles, perhaps you are right about the feel of a place. Perhaps we are mistaken to attempt to settle near Bath, and your dismay is a way of indicating that we are looking in the wrong neighborhood. What do you think of continuing our search in Derbyshire, where the feel of Pemberley might be easier to obtain?"

"Derbyshire is known for its beauty. I dare say it might possess just what I am looking for," Bingley said, cheering at the idea.

"Very well, then. We shall seek a leased estate that feels like Pemberley," she said soothingly, pleased at her ability to restore sibling harmony quickly.

"Yes, let Pemberley be my guide," Bingley murmured.

"A trip to Pemberley would help me understand what it is you are seeking," Caroline urged. Bingley had often spoken of his desire that she see Pemberley, but he was slow to take action. She possessed only a budding friendship with the handsome Darcy and his darling sister, formed after a brief introduction at the tail end of last season in London.

Summoning her sweetest tone, she inquired. "I suppose such a visit is not possible?"

"Of course, it is possible!" Bingley asserted, his brow furrowing as he railed against the implied suggestion that his friendship with Darcy was too shallow to allow for impromptu visits. "I have been to Pemberley many times and always feel terribly welcome. The trouble is, I do not know if Darcy is currently at home."

"Well, you are his friend and know him best. I cannot initiate a call on my own. It would seem a shame to not meet up at last when we are already on the road and have no other obligations," she said slyly.

"Yes, you may be right that I should take a chance and make an effort," Bingley replied with renewed enthusiasm. "I will write to him immediately."

Once back in their comfortable rooms at 7 Paragon, he settled the matter within himself. He vowed not to put his signature to a lease unless it felt like Pemberley. Pleased with himself and beset by the memory of his pleasant visits in Derbyshire, he penned a brief letter to Darcy to inquire if he were at home and if he were amenable to a visit by the four of them. He had the footman post the letter immediately and, not holding out much hope for a speedy reply, promptly put the matter out of his mind.

***

"I do hope that horrid Mr. Waxman is not there this evening, Louisa," Caroline whined as she cut daintily into her beef that night at dinner. "For I hope that I am not so unfortunate to have collected only one suitor during our time in Bath, and an ugly specimen at that."

"Try not to be so pleasant to him then," Mr. Hurst advised, swirling the burgundy in his glass.

"But being pleasant is so natural to me," Caroline lamented.

"I have the same problem," Mrs. Hurst concurred. They exchanged glances and nodded at each other.

"Excessive good humor is our family way," Bingley agreed in earnest, glancing up at the candelabra that hung over the dining table. "Is it dim in here or is it me?"

"It's not you. There are not enough candles to light this place sufficiently. I can barely see my food," Mr. Hurst noted. "Cheap tapers for the price they extort for this place," he snorted.

"Yes, it could be brighter lit," Caroline agreed. "That is the problem with a seasonal lease. But I ask you, seriously, who comes to

Bath to meet a man with a dark, long beard smelling of tobacco when there are so many handsome, finely dressed young gentlemen one sees everywhere in passing? Have I no hope to be introduced to some of the clever young things?"

Bath had disappointed Miss Bingley. "I don't know what I was expecting," she sighed, but even as the words escaped her, she knew them to be false. She had fallen into the sad habit of comparing every new acquaintance to Mr. Darcy, and thus, every new acquaintance was found lacking.

"You must learn to be more cutting with your acquaintances. Society is a tricky thing. It must be *managed* if you are to make a quality match," Mrs. Hurst advised, waving her fork at her sister for emphasis.

"Then tonight, I must be willing to sacrifice an evening of dancing should Mr. Waxman insist on approaching me," Caroline mused. "For I do not wish to be seen with him so often. I only wish to be seen associating with a *particular* type of gentleman."

"Do you really despair of Bath society, so? I find the company delightful," Bingley said, looking at her with incredulity as he chewed.

Mrs. Hurst pointed her plump finger at her brother. "You, my dear, would do well to be more discriminating in your dance partners. Tarts are all I see swarming around you." She dabbed the corners of her mouth with her linen napkin.

"Really, Louisa, I simply don't see it!" Bingley objected, turning crimson and looking to Caroline for support.

Caroline tilted her head but diplomatically refused to take a side. Her siblings seemed to stumble through life without any sort of a plan. Charles fell in and out of love quite often, and Louisa was securely married to the son of their late father's partner, who was the first man to ever pay her attention. Caroline, however, could not be so carefree. Her wants were specific, and her aim was high. A spouse possessing more than her own twenty thousand pounds and a country estate were her minimum requirements. A London house would be lovely but could always be purchased during the marriage. A title would be the topper, but trickier for her to achieve when her family's fortune was acquired by trade.

"Eh, let him have his fun," Mr. Hurst snorted, smiling at Bingley. "He knows better than to marry one of 'em, don't you, lad?"

Bingley reddened and stabbed at his beef.

***

That night, as Caroline feared, the hirsute Mr. Waxman approached as soon as she entered the Upper Rooms.

"Miss Bingley, the honor of the first two dances?" His hot breath hung in the air between them.

Caroline held her breath to prevent inhaling his trademark scent. She said stiffly, "I am sorry, but I do not intend to dance tonight."

Surprised by her refusal, he grimaced and stared trout-like at her in a dumbfounded manner. Then, rightly sensing defeat, he backed away and was subsumed into the crowd.

Satisfied with the efficiency of her rebuff, Caroline took her seat against the wall. She was content to amuse herself by criticizing the gowns, complexions, and desperation of that night's assembled. An hour in, she watched with delight as the dreadful Mr. Waxman formed an attachment to a portly, middle-aged widow rumored to have an estate on the Welsh coast.

"Well done, Caroline," Mrs. Hurst said from behind her silk fan.

Caroline smiled back smugly.

"It had to be done. Now, of a separate concern, those Hanover sisters are entirely too invested tonight in our Bingley." She made an imperceptible nod toward the right side of the room where the two young ladies had Bingley cornered.

"They must have discovered his hundred thousand," Mrs. Hurst snickered. "For I saw them here last night, stuck like dried porridge to that toad Mr. Simpson and paying no heed to Bingley. Mr. Simpson is said to have money, but not what our Bingley has. Now look how they buzz around Bingley like flies."

"He seems entirely too delighted in their attention," Mrs. Hurst observed. "Yes, they are pretty in a rough way. I'd say tolerable at best if you are in the hinterlands, but they barely pass for gentility in a town like Bath."

"I shall have another word with him," Caroline said with an edge of determination in her tone. Bingley's propensity to fall for this young lady or that without regard to pedigree kept Caroline on her toes. "And if he cannot quit them, then *we* will simply quit Bath. It is easy enough to come up with an urgent need to move on, and Bingley will put up no argument."

Mrs. Hurst nodded in implicit agreement.

"I expected better prospects from the assembled," Caroline said after a moment's continued observation. "Why is everyone so coarse-looking? Is there not one person here of wealth and breeding whose society we could latch onto for advancement? Is there no one *interesting* here at all?"

Mrs. Hurst shrugged her shoulders and said with disapprobation, "Were such a woman present, I doubt Bingley would be drawn to her. He lacks discrimination. It is his greatest fault."

"I fear for Bingley," Caroline confessed. "You are correct in saying he is indiscriminate. So much can go wrong so quickly with him if we are not careful."

# *CHAPTER TWO*

One week later, Miss Bingley and Mrs. Hurst promenaded through Sydney Gardens. Bingley's sisters spent liberally while in town, and they took to the gardens with equal degrees of pride in their appearance and desperation to be noticed. The paths were busy, and the assembled ladies respectable and dressed for show. The garden, filled with romantic vistas, sham castles, and shady alcoves for moments of respite, was so extensive that traversing it could dispense with two to three otherwise very dull hours of the day.

Bingley's flirtation with the Hanover sisters had continued unabated and preoccupied their thoughts.

"Did you see how they hovered about Bingley at last night's concert?" Caroline asked.

"How could I miss it? Their compliments are cloying," Louisa answered.

"I asked around and confirmed my suspicions; their connections are beyond low—a waste of our residency here. I do not believe it premature of me to have decided it is time to move on," Caroline said firmly.

"I hear Surrey is picturesque," Mrs. Hurst suggested.

"Yes, it has that reputation. But I have another idea," she

replied, unable to contain a smile.

"Oh? Do you? I recognize that look. What are you up to?" Mrs. Hurst laughed.

"What look?" Caroline asked, keeping her gaze focused ahead of her.

"You know what look. You obviously have an idea that you are bursting to tell me," Mrs. Hurst insisted.

Caroline sighed. "It is thankless work maneuvering this family into the right society. And do watch where you are going, sister," she said, guiding Mrs. Hurst slightly off the path to sidestep an oncoming matron.

"Thank you. That was a close call," Mrs. Hurst said. "That old cow saw me coming but didn't yield in the slightest. I'm sorry. Do continue. I agree with you about leaving Bath. But where to next?"

"Derbyshire," Caroline announced decidedly.

"Derbyshire?"

"Yes," Caroline said as she flushed a hint of pink.

"Oh, I see," Mrs. Hurst said in a gentle tone. "It's Darcy, isn't it? It's always been Darcy."

"He is everything I want, Louisa. Tall, genteel, possessing a home in London and a country seat renowned for its beauty. How can I sit still in such a place as this—a place filled with Mr. Waxmans and Hanover tarts—when Mr. Darcy is in the world?"

"Then you must win him," Mrs. Hurst responded with conviction.

"But can I, I wonder?" Caroline admitted in a rare moment of doubt. "I have a feeling that with him it is not so easy. If it were, I believe some social-climbing beauty would have claimed him by now."

"Fiddlesticks," Mrs. Hurst said in a low scolding tone. "There is no shame in social climbing. Of course you can win him. Why he is only a man, and we both know that men are very easily swayed. Look at Charles and Mr. Hurst, for instance."

"And Father as well,' Caroline nodded.

"What is the name of Darcy's country pile again?"

"Pemberley."

"Ah, Pemberley. Bingley must take us there! They are beyond good friends."

"Bingley did write to Darcy inquiring. He was rhapsodizing so about Pemberley that I believe he lost all perspective and foolishly rejected that perfectly suitable Carlisle House. I had to remind him that Pemberley isn't for sale. But," Caroline said with a wry smile, "I did easily convince him to redirect our search for a country home to Derbyshire. Of course, I had my own motives for making such a suggestion."

"Very clever girl, you are. What a fun game it will be to win over Darcy. Our biggest challenge yet."

"Oh, Louisa, no," Caroline suddenly whispered, and she grasped Mrs. Hurst's arm to stop her. But it was too late. Mr. Waxman was directly ahead of them on the gravel path, and he had spotted them first.

He oiled up to Caroline and smiled directly at her, seemingly unconscious that she meant to cut him at the assembly.

"Miss Bingley, Mrs. Hurst. How pleasant to see you both," he smiled at the ladies, but his gaze lingered on Caroline.

Caroline stiffened. "Good day, Mr. Waxman."

"I look forward to the next time we see each other at the assembly rooms. I have not given up on the idea of those dances, Miss Bingley."

"Mr. Waxman, you are too kind," Caroline lied.

"Will you be there tonight?"

"Oh, I am sorry," Mrs. Hurst replied. "We are engaged for tonight. Tomorrow night at the earliest."

"Then I will look for you starting tomorrow. Good day, ladies," he tipped his hat and smiled.

Caroline nodded coolly and both ladies walked on without comment, until Mrs. Hurst said, "What dreadful bad luck to run into him."

Caroline sighed. "Now I understand him to be dense as well as unattractive. I am more determined than ever to quit this place."

"I understand your urgency," Mrs. Hurst whispered back.

Thus agreed, they returned to Paragon, separating as they entered the home—Mrs. Hurst climbing the stairs to her room and Caroline making her way to the drawing room where she found Bingley. He was sitting on the window seat, engrossed in a letter, a smile plastered on his sunlit face.

"Good afternoon! What is so pleasing that you hardly

noticed my entrance?" Caroline exclaimed as she crossed into the room.

Bingley looked up. "Forgive me. It is only a letter from Darcy."

"Mr. Darcy of Pemberley, the home above all homes?" Caroline teased, sitting down and straightening her skirts about her. Her heart beat several times faster to speak Darcy's name aloud.

"Yes, my old chum."

"And what is his news?" Caroline asked with studied disinterest.

"You will be pleased to know he has invited us to join him to stay at Pemberley, immediately, if possible. It appears that Miss Darcy is home with him unexpectedly, and she is greatly in need of companionship."

"How wonderful. Bingley, we must not refuse him. We can continue our hunt for a place there."

Bingley frowned. "Unfortunately, I don't see how we can leave now, as we are committed to our lease here."

"Committed?" Caroline asked archly. "Why use such a strong word?"

There they were in Bath, struggling to connect with people of quality. Why would they refuse an invitation from the best people of their acquaintance? Bingley could be so daft and managing him so tiresome. Lately, she found herself longing for a brother who actually gave a thought to her advancement in society instead of leaving it all to chance.

"What? No … I mean, I thought you … "Bingley stammered, confused. "But we paid upfront for the lease to secure these rooms. Positively no refunds."

"But of course, we will go to Pemberley! Never mind the money, we have plenty.  It sounds as if your friend is in real need, and I simply cannot allow you to refuse his request. Write him directly and accept," she said.

Bingley, somewhat astonished by his sister's forceful reaction, took a moment to move to his desk, and in that moment, Caroline impatiently rang the bell for the footman. Upon his entering, she stated, "We are quitting Bath tomorrow. Mr. Bingley will give you further instructions."

With that, she strode swiftly out of the room and started up the staircase crying out, "Louisa! Louisa! The most exciting news!"

# *CHAPTER THREE*

"Miss Darcy, you are wanted by the master," the housemaid said.

Georgiana looked up from her sketchpad. She sat on the window seat in her sitting room, drawing out ideas for a new table and gazing out the window at the rows of oaks and Spanish chestnuts that lined Pemberley's long drive. Upon her arrival home from Ramsgate, she had taken a liking to the rarely used room, and her brother could not have been kinder in fitting it up for her as fashionably as possible. He even encouraged her to sketch out her own designs for new furniture, which he was more than happy to commission.

"Coming," she said obediently as she put down her pad and pencil. She stood and smoothed down her skirt then followed the maid past the great hall and then to the main drawing room where her brother waited. Once inside, her eye was drawn to where Darcy stood silhouetted against the window, and she gasped. A harp, long desired by Georgiana, stood next to him.

"Do you like it?" Darcy asked, eager for her reaction.

"You didn't!" Georgiana exclaimed, her hand flying to her heart in surprise.

"Yes, I did," Darcy answered proudly. "Come, take a look at it."

Georgiana had never seen an instrument so light in style and construction as the one displayed before her.

"Is it ours?" she inquired, unable to hide the hope in her tone.

"Yes, it's yours. And lessons included, of course."

"You are too kind," she cried, running to him and throwing her arms around him in an embrace. He returned her embrace, holding her tightly.

"Sit down and try it," he urged her, his voice cracking with emotion.

Georgiana pulled up the accompanying stool and arranged herself nervously before the instrument. She hesitated. Then, timidly, she drew her hand across the strings.

Darcy's eyes lit up with a mixture of brotherly pride and affection. "Beautiful."

She met his gaze and then returned her concentration to the instrument, drawing her fingers across the strings with increasing energy. "Oh, Fitzwilliam!" she shook her head. "I promise to practice daily so that I will be worthy of your largesse."

"Father and Mother would have done twice as much for you," he said. He stood silently and watched Georgiana gently pluck at the strings, real delight shining from her eyes. A thrill of satisfaction surged within him; he loved nothing more than to spoil his sister.

"And I'm sorry about the singing lessons. Miss Canton's suggested replacement was not suitable," he said.

Georgiana barely looked up. "I'll be busy with my harp." She had been disappointed to lose her voice tutor, but her brother was right. They would wait for a replacement that met Darcy's qualifications. She understood why her brother turned down the young man who came for an interview; once inside Pemberley, he increased his fee substantially. Darcy didn't want another mercenary like Wickham near their home.

The harp, an extravagance Darcy had long resisted, came at the perfect time. He feared that Georgiana's stay that summer was lacking in pleasant distractions. Therefore, Darcy had thanked heaven when he received Bingley's unexpected letter explaining that he and his sisters were currently stationed in Bath but were now interested in exploring potential estates to lease in Derbyshire and could he possibly impose by coming to visit?

Yes, Darcy had thought immediately. The company of the familiar, high-spirited Bingley would distract and entertain Georgiana.

And himself.

He and Georgiana had been too much on their own. Col. Fitzwilliam was expected at Pemberley later to check in on his charge and to lend necessary support. But other than that hopeful prospect, Pemberley was too quiet for their taste; company was necessary.

He had learned a hard lesson over the summer—his sister was not a child anymore. She needed the right society and proper companions, and it was his responsibility to ensure that happened.

But he concurred that he did not require society's best; he only required society he could trust.

Who better than old friends?

He harbored a secret hope that Bingley and Georgiana would form a connection. He had never thought of the match before, but Wickham's treachery had forced him to consider the type of man whom he would wish Georgiana to marry. Safe was the word that kept coming to mind, and Bingley was the definition of safe. With his own wealth, Bingley had no need to fortune-hunt.

Matchmaking aside, at the very least, Bingley's sisters would prove useful companions for Georgiana. The Bingley sisters were familiar and frivolous and perfect distractions. He had quite enjoyed their company the few times they had met in London as they were surprisingly well-educated, he thought, despite their Northern origins.

Soon an express from Bath brought glad tidings—the Bingley party was quitting its rooms and would be on their way immediately. The news sent the Pemberley staff into a flurry of delightful anticipation. The estate was at its best with a houseful.

"I must remember to tell Bingley to check out Chipperton House to lease," Darcy said as he and Georgiana sat before the evening fire.

She looked up from her stitch work. "Is he looking?"

"Apparently so. Chipperton is but four miles down the road. I am not sure what his taste is, but I will encourage him to check it out. I can think of nothing better than to have good friends situated close by."

"Chipperton has been around forever. I remember the picnics Mr. Trent used to host. I am sure Bingley will take it."

Darcy smiled back at Georgiana. She seemed perfectly content as she sat humming and stitching. Perhaps he was letting her mistake at Ramsgate weigh on him too much. Wickham was dutifully banished, Georgiana convincingly warned off of future louts, and good friends were already on the road, heading their way. It was high summertime, and the Derbyshire countryside was at its peak. He was the master of Pemberley with very little to fear and everything to look forward to. He smiled back at his sister and, for the first time in what felt like weeks, breathed a deep sigh of relief.

***

At noon on the day of their expected arrival, Bingley's coach approached the turnoff to Pemberley. As the foliage cleared and the house came into view, Caroline Bingley finally got her long-awaited look at Pemberley. It was more impressive than she had imagined, and her hopes for a future with Darcy were inflamed by the expanse and grandeur displayed before her.

Nevertheless, she was canny enough to temper her enthusiasm. It would not help her position to seem overly impressed by their way of life. And so, after the initial swell of greetings and a leisurely lunch, she followed along on the house tour led by Darcy and was careful to display no outward indication of how rapidly her eager heart beat with excitement. Down the long galleries, up the broad staircase, past chamber after chamber and room after room designed for comfort and ease, she smiled serenely and murmured how lovely it all was and how delighted they were to be there. Yet all the while, her mathematical mind was calculating the enormous value of everything she saw.

Later that night, as she blew out the candle at her bedside and tucked herself under the silky spread, she understood her brother's fascination with Pemberley and why he sought to replicate it in their own lives. She had been there less than a day but could already see that life at Pemberley was the perfect mix of grandeur and gentility. Miss Darcy was a diamond and Darcy the consummate squire.

Furthermore, if she attended every ball in every county, she could not find a more appropriate match for Bingley than Georgiana Darcy. Caroline shuddered, remembering the Hanover ladies in their cheap gowns. She imagined the inevitability of Georgiana and Bingley falling for each other during their stay.

And Darcy!

Now there was a man of substance, the likes of whom would not be seen loitering in a common dance hall in Bath. His manner was not as amiable as Bingley's, but few men were, she decided. She sighed deeply and retraced their tour of Pemberley in her mind. Oh, to be in possession of so much silk and crystal, and a man as commanding as he.

With her own high style and Darcy's dark good looks, the two of them could usher in a new era of glamour at Pemberley. They would be known throughout the county for the splendor of their society and their charity. She pulled the quilt closer and whispered to herself, "The first night in my future home."

***

Happy were the warm summer weeks the two families spent together at Pemberley. They ventured out every day, taking their daily turns touring the gardens, exploring the nearby peaks and valleys, picnicking by the shimmering inland lakes, or following winding paths past moss-covered stone fences. When they tired of their exertions and sat indoors, the lilting notes of the harp were their constant companion as Georgiana pursued her lessons with equal parts discipline and determination.

They dined each night on fresh game and lettuces culled from Pemberley's fertile farms. With the candles lit and the windows thrown open to the night air, life at Pemberley had a hint of magic to it. There was a golden glow to the rooms quite like nothing Caroline had ever seen, and so different from the cheaply furnished tourist rentals of Bath.

Bingley and Darcy fell into their old ways, riding out each afternoon to call on tenants or survey the crops, returning in time for Mrs. Reynold's iced buns and coffee or tea—a treat she had prepared since her master and mistress were young children. Bingley doted on Darcy's dogs and, after consuming the late afternoon tea repast, took to nodding off in contentment, his head resting comfortably on the old, down-filled cushions while the fresh country air blew in through the open windows.

Several times a week, Caroline, Mrs. Hurst, and Miss Darcy would call for the carriage and ride into nearby Lambton to visit the shops. Both Bingley sisters found the town delightful; its charming shops offering a selection of stylish and pricey wares. They would always stop to take tea and hear the news in the local tea house, which was a cozy and elegant establishment. Caroline could not help but notice that everywhere they went, Miss Darcy was afforded a deference that Caroline envied.

Like her brother, Caroline found herself falling deeper and deeper under the spell of Pemberley's rural charms. And, she laughed to herself, the alluring presence of its handsome owner.

But despite her high expectations, Caroline quickly deduced that Darcy, though impeccably mannered, showed her no partiality. There was no luster in his eyes when he gazed her way, nor did she catch him studying her when she was unaware. He displayed no evidence of enchantment.

She sighed deeply.

If passion would not compel Darcy to choose her as his wife, then she was just as willing for him to pick her by default. In the end, it would produce the same result. She therefore vowed to prove her worth in her daily faithfulness to him, taking note of all his preferences so that she could please him. Her plan was to always be in proximity to him, so constant a part of his daily life that he could no longer imagine his life without her.

None of which she could do from afar. It fell to Bingley to

help make that happen by leasing an estate in Derbyshire as soon as possible. Her ascension to mistress of Pemberley rested on that detail.

Heeding Darcy's recommendation, Bingley willingly made an appointment to view Chipperton House, and he extended invitations to all to ride along with him.

The Hursts regretfully declined, promising to make the trip if the place proved promising, but Georgiana and Caroline were more than pleased to join their respective brothers on the outing. On the day of the appointment, the foursome happily drove away in the open carriage, bathed in sunlight with a slight breeze at their backs. All were secretly hopeful and confident that Chipperton House would mark the beginning of the next chapter of their lives.

Chipperton House was four miles southwest of the gates of Pemberley via the main artery. The drive there was picturesque—all blue sky and dark green hedgerows that framed more green valleys. When at last the property came into view, Caroline and Georgiana exclaimed at its fineness. The structure was decades old and well-settled into the landscape.

Upon meeting the steward, he led them inside. The party admired the artistry of the home's carved banisters, the massive chimneypieces, the strapwork and paneling, and its sturdy furnishings. Both Miss Darcy and Miss Bingley noted the enchanting view of the gardens seen through the mullioned windows.

Darcy remarked on the well-kept outbuildings and the fact that the roof was in good repair. A stream cut across the northern tip of the property providing ample opportunity to fish, the steward noted, a fact that pleased both men. Yet throughout the entirety of the tour, Bingley remained uncharacteristically quiet.

When at last they congregated back outside and the steward left them alone to discuss their impressions, all were uniform in their approval.

Only Bingley demurred.

"It's a little Elizabethan, wouldn't you say?" Bingley said at last, his gaze taking in the width of the old I.

"You are correct. Good eye," Darcy commended him.

"I don't know that I like it," Bingley said.

Surprised and alarmed at his negativity, Caroline could not contain her irritation.

"Oh Charles, don't be such a snob," she snapped. "What did you think of the size of the rooms and the beautiful grounds? Doesn't it feel very much like Pemberley? I thought so."

"No," Charles said with a frown, shaking his head and sticking his hands in his coat pocket. "Not to me. It is quite dark inside. It's a bright day but not in there."

Caroline and Darcy exchanged bemused glances. His stubborn dismissal of the place concerned them, as neither had anticipated a fight.

But, Caroline remembered, it was only Bingley. He was always easily swayed.

"Miss Darcy," Caroline began. "You are equally impressed with Chipperton—I can see from the look on your face that you think it lovely. Do tell Bingley how lucky we are to have this opportunity."

Miss Darcy smiled politely at Miss Bingley but was more moved by Bingley's complaint and sided with him.

"Yes, Mr. Bingley, I see what you mean. The Elizabethan architecture does feel dated now; I would not choose the period myself. And the furniture is in need of updating. Without a considerable investment in upgrading the décor, its best days are behind it."

Bingley shot a winsome smile at Miss Darcy, grateful for her encouragement.

Although impressed by Miss Darcy's wife-like support of Bingley, Caroline was visibly vexed to see his veto encouraged, and she sought to steer him to her point of view.

"But the setting is perfect. I have never seen such natural beauty. Were you to lease it and find favor with it, in time you could purchase the property and make it over in a more modern style," Caroline urged.

"I had not thought of that," Bingley said, rubbing his nose nervously. He thoughtfully studied the façade of the old manor house for a few moments.

Turning back to the group, he asked with genuine curiosity, "But what is the point, may I ask, of buying a property one does not care for? Why not wait until one finds the perfect place?"

Caroline said impatiently, "There is no perfect place, only perfect settings. Your feelings about the house be what they may, but

I must emphasize that this setting is delightful, and I would hate for you to act rashly in refusing it."

Bingley stood quietly in the face of his sister's impassioned plea, inwardly frustrated. Darcy read the expression on his friend's face and felt for him.

"Sleep on it," Darcy advised in a gentle tone. "You may change your mind. You may find something to like in its Elizabethan quality after all. And if not, there will be other options."

Bingley nodded. Darcy always made the most sense to him of anybody, and he never regretted taking his old friend's advice. Bingley sighed noticeably and promised not to rule it out.

They thanked the steward and climbed back into the carriage to return to Pemberley. Immediately upon disembarking, Darcy asked for the horses. He and Bingley and Mr. Hurst then set off on their customary afternoon ride around the estate.

Tired from their excursion, the young ladies settled in the drawing room. Miss Darcy gravitated back to the harp while the Bingley sisters waited for tea.

"Miss Darcy, your playing improves every day," Caroline said.

"Thank you, Miss Bingley. I am new to the instrument, and my feeble attempts to master it must prove to be a great annoyance to your ears."

Miss Bingley waved away Georgiana's concerns. "Nonsense. Even your missed notes are a delight. Oh, I do hope my brother comes to his senses and leases Chipperton. How nice it will be for us to remain in the neighborhood." Caroline smiled across the room, but Miss Darcy did not catch it; her head was downturned, concentrating on the strings.

"What was wrong with the place?" Mrs. Hurst inquired lazily.

"Too Elizabethan," Caroline said with a roll of her eyes. "Who knew Charles was an architecture snob?"

"He is only leasing. If he is displeased, he can move on," Mrs. Hurst said, picking up on her sister's frustration.

"My advice exactly," Caroline nodded. "Of course, there may be other estates in the county more pleasing to my brother's exacting aesthetic standards," she said with sarcasm, "but I cannot imagine that there are very many at such a convenient proximity to Pemberley. How I have grown to love this area."

"I am so glad you admire it," Georgiana said sweetly, halting her practice momentarily in surprise at Caroline's sarcasm toward Bingley. She hoped that Caroline and her brother would not dig in on their disagreement regarding Chipperton; Georgiana abhorred sibling unrest. However, she did not despair over Bingley's failure to find pleasure in the place as Caroline did.

In a spirit of encouragement, Georgiana looked at Caroline and said, "Do not fret about Chipperton. It is an old home in need of much repair. There are many lovely homes in the district. I am sure the right one will become available in time; perhaps in a year or two?"

Caroline bristled at the idea.

*A year or two?*

She did not have a year or two to waste when there was a perfectly sensible solution right in front of them. In a year or two

Darcy could be married to someone else. Still, she hid her annoyance and sweetly murmured, "Perhaps you are right."

Anxious for a less turbulent topic of conversation, Caroline directed her gaze upward at the ornately framed ancestral portraits lining the soaring walls. Rising, she strolled over to them, skimming the engraved names on the brass plates until she came to the one she hoped to find.

"So, this was your mother," Caroline observed.

Georgiana looked up. "Yes."

"I can see her expression and her dark coloring in Darcy—your hair is much lighter, but you share the same eye color?" Caroline studied Georgiana's fawn colored-hair and blue eyes.

"So everyone says," Georgiana agreed.

Caroline studied the portrait—Lady Anne was finely dressed in a cornflower blue gown; a pearl comb adorned her dark curls. The portrait had captured both her dignity and her innate warmth.

Georgiana stood up from the harp and stepped softly across the room to stand next to Caroline and gazed up at her mother's portrait with evident pleasure. "She's wearing her signature blue. It was her favorite color."

"Was it?" Caroline replied.

"Yes, so many of her gowns are some shade of blue. It matched her eyes."

"Yes, I can see that now," Caroline agreed, studying the portrait. The silk gown and its trimmings were the fashion of a previous generation, but the iridescent pearl comb adorning Lady

Darcy's dark hair was a classic. Caroline committed the shape of the comb to her memory.

"We are a lot alike," Georgiana said softly as they stared up at the image of the last mistress of Pemberley.

"You and your mother?" Caroline said. "I'm not surprised."

"No," Georgiana said. "I meant you and me." Georgiana grasped Caroline's hand as she spoke and squeezed it gently.

Caroline was confused at her meaning. "You mean we dress alike?"

"No," Georgiana shook her head slightly. "I mean that we are both motherless and at the mercy of our brothers' comings and goings. Both with uncertain futures."

Caroline nodded soberly at Georgiana's statement.

"I see. I never thought about us that way," Caroline said, and she gave Georgiana a quick squeeze in response, not caring to disagree outwardly.

For disagree she did with Georgiana's I assessment, as Caroline saw clearly what Georgiana did not. Darcy was a man of considerable conviction—a man who had proven to have his sister's best interest at heart. Darcy was the kind of man who would see the good in settling in a place like Chipperton and look beyond his own peculiar whims to make wise decisions beneficial to the whole family. Whereas Bingley, albeit an agreeable man, was driven by his own shifting impulses and would pass on a desirable lease due to a silly notion about architectural preference.

No, Georgiana, we are not alike, she thought. I would be

lucky to have a brother who cared about my future as much as your brother cares about yours.

# *CHAPTER FOUR*

Privately, Caroline did not concede to Bingley's whims, and she continued to pressure him into leasing Chipperton.

"Please take another look at your leisure," she urged him. "Perhaps it will not disappoint you so much upon second glance. I do so love the area, and how often will a suitable accommodation be available?"

"But I do not wish to keep disturbing the steward. He was generous enough with his time already," Bingley argued.

"Please, consider what the whole family might gain were we to be regular fixtures in Pemberley society," she hinted. Bingley, however, remained firm. "It does not have the feel that I want."

"But how can you be so sure? You were the one who thought Derbyshire felt like home," she said, purposely twisting his words. "Can't you imagine yourself there? I can."

"No, I can't. I'll take another ride past it, if you insist, but I'm not going in," he said, hoping to mollify her.

Recognizing defeat, Caroline stomped away, silently seething at her brother's stubborn refusal.

Darcy, too, was secretly disappointed that his friend was so decided against the place. He would have loved the companionship.

He found Bingley's family to be very pleasant company. Mr. Hurst was as genial as Bingley and a solid extra man, always up for a card game or a round of shooting.

Then there was the prospect of Bingley and Georgiana marrying.

The two seemed to get on quite easily with each other, and having Bingley settled at Chipperton might accelerate a match. However, Bingley, who had been known to declare himself in love five minutes after an introduction, had not yet exhibited any symptoms of lovesickness since arriving at Pemberley.

Indeed, the lion's share of Bingley's affection was slathered on Darcy's dogs.

Separately, Darcy advised the frustrated Caroline not to despair.

"Bingley is engaging in a rare display of stubbornness. As it is not his nature, I am hopeful we may still change his mind," Darcy remarked.

"I have tried, Mr. Darcy. He is unyielding," Caroline answered.

"Give him time. Give me a chance to work on him," he said with a look of earnestness that Caroline could not help but read into.

"Whatever you could do would be greatly appreciated," she smiled back.

"I will make another round of inquiries in the neighborhood as well. I cannot imagine it too hard to find something to tempt your brother."

"I do hope you are right."

"As for now, say nothing to disturb him."

"I promise," she replied.

***

On his part, Darcy was more than pleased with the turn Georgiana's summer had taken. He thought that Bingley's sisters rounded out the house party quite amusingly, and their presence had distracted both he and Georgiana from their recent distress. Often, Georgiana's laughter could be heard echoing throughout the halls of Pemberley, and his worries about his sister dissipated as easily as the morning dew.

Although their roots were in the northern trade towns, Darcy appreciated that Miss Bingley and Mrs. Hurst were women of quality. Both had benefitted from a private seminary education, could hold a conversation with assurance, and had mastery of French and Italian languages. Mrs. Hurst was as cheerful and unassuming as her brother.

Caroline, however, had a willful streak to her that surprised him. It was the kind of steely character needed to rule a place like Pemberley, he believed. He thought her no great beauty, but she was well-groomed and fashionable enough for Derbyshire's society; she was obviously eligible and would be an easy conquest.

He seriously debated pursuing a courtship between them that would lead to a proposal. But the more he mused on the topic, the more torn he found himself. Darcy was in the habit of assessing all young ladies that came into his circle, and by the end of their first week together, he concluded that while Caroline possessed much common sense as well as an ability to command respect from those around her, she inspired no great feeling in him.

He did not ever think of her when she was not in the same room, and he had a firm conviction that his future wife should occupy his thoughts with a ferocity that shook the ground beneath him.

However, he was sensible to the fact that for some lucky people, friendship sometimes blossomed into a love capable of lasting a lifetime. For this reason, he thought it prudent to keep Miss Bingley close but at arm's length. She was eager to please and utterly transparent in her desire to be mistress of Pemberley—a goal he was always careful not to encourage.

He felt the great weight of choosing the right spouse for himself and thought that, on this issue, it would be wise for him to seek the advice of someone he trusted deeply—his cousin, Col. Fitzwilliam.

Darcy had frankly described the disastrous chain of events at Ramsgate to Col. Fitzwilliam, with whom he shared guardianship of his sister. Upon hearing the news, Col. Fitzwilliam felt strongly that he should come to Pemberley in order to better share Darcy's burden at such a tender time. He quickly rearranged his affairs and made the necessary arrangements to arrive at Pemberley late summer.

Darcy put his thoughts on Miss Bingley aside until he could discuss the matter in person with his cousin, who always had the best advice, he thought.

Colonel Fitzwilliam arrived on a Thursday and his cousins warmly greeted him. Col. Fitzwilliam was an easy-going man and upon introduction to Bingley and his family, with whom he was unfamiliar, fell easily into a rapport with the company. They all stayed up well past midnight on his first night, playing hand after hand of whist until Mr. Hurst fell fast asleep on the games table and could not be budged.

Yet despite the bonhomie that Col. Fitzwilliam exuded, Caroline immediately noticed a change in the air. After the initial warm welcome, tense conversations ensued, held behind closed doors. Col. Fitzwilliam's demeanor remained calm, but his very presence seemed to bring to the surface some matter that troubled Darcy and Georgiana equally. Whatever the nature of the trouble, Darcy was careful to conceal it. Caroline watched and wondered, keeping her suspicions to herself. She knew better than to ask questions.

Yet if Caroline thought her watchful ways went unnoticed, she was mistaken. Darcy was her match in reading a room, and it did not escape his attention that Caroline Bingley seemed to be unusually silent as of late.

Deathly silent.

The better to overhear what was meant to be private.

Her presence required Darcy to limit his conversations regarding Georgiana to the outdoors. A few days after his arrival, he invited Col. Fitzwilliam to accompany him on an afternoon walk to the orchard. He desired to add another acre or so and wanted his cousin's opinion on that and the more sensitive topic of Miss Bingley. But before Darcy could open up, Col. Fitzwilliam made a suggestion.

"I would like to take Georgiana to Rosings with me for an extended stay," he offered. "There is no safer environment for her than Rosings, and the distraction of her aunt's and cousin's company will be beneficial. Additionally, it will give you a needed break. I am not unaware of the anxiety this episode has caused; it is etched on your face."

Darcy's first reaction was to refuse the suggestion. He was not so affected by Wickham's wicked ways as to be rendered ineffective in his duties toward Georgiana. But he was a proponent of the physical and mental benefits derived from a change of scene and company. And Lady Catherine was always writing that Georgiana should stay more at Rosings than she currently did. His sister needed a feminine influence, Lady Catherine often said, and she had warned Darcy that Georgiana spent too much time with hired companions.

His aunt was a formidable presence, quick to criticize, and so he had chosen *not* to inform her of Wickham's treachery. Nevertheless, her general advice and guidance might be useful at present.

For Georgiana's sake, he could not refuse the offer.

"Thank you, dear cousin," Darcy said. "My only concern is that Georgiana be safe and happy. Knowing she is under your care at Rosings will be a relief."

"My thoughts exactly. Anne will be a trustworthy companion. And, as the society in Rosings is very fine, we have no worry about the quality of the people she may be exposed to there."

"I do not fear a repeat of Ramsgate. Georgiana is quite shaken by the close call and has promised never to conceal her connections from me again. She is so afraid of making a misstep. I do believe her when she says this will not be a pattern. But, going forward, she may well benefit from the feminine counsel of my aunt. I have not written to her of the affair in Ramsgate, have you?"

"No," Col. Fitzwilliam confirmed.

"Very well. I say continue on as we have in that regard. But I will write and accept her invitation," Darcy decided.

"Very good," Col. Fitzwilliam breathed in the warm afternoon scent of ripening apples as the orchard neared. "Enjoy your time then with your houseguests when we are gone. I am sure you will be on our minds greatly, as Aunt Catherine will go on about your duty to marry her Anne, no matter how strong the evidence to the contrary continues to be."

"Discouragement issued from my own lips does little to dissuade her hopes. I fear she will continue to live in this fantasy of her own making until the end of her days," Darcy shook his head.

"She forgets you are a grown man with your own strong will. I believe she will always think of you as her little nephew whose future she wants to control," Col. Fitzwilliam agreed. "May I be so bold as to inquire if the young lady, Miss Bingley, is more than a friend?"

Darcy shook his head. "As of yet, no. She is a breath of fresh air. Her figure is elegant, and her character possesses the best parts of her brother's but with a decidedness to her temperament that is appealing."

"I wish you luck then."

"No luck is needed, thank you, but I am desirous of your opinion. She is pleasant company for now, and her interest in me, or may I state more correctly, interest in Pemberley, is obvious."

"But? Do I sense hesitation on your end?"

"Yes. I am presently not inclined to marry but am conscious of the opportunity before me. I would prefer to wait to marry. In five years, when Georgiana is older, then the time would be ideal."

"The young Miss Bingley will most certainly not care to wait five years without encouragement," Col. Fitzwilliam replied with a slight lift of his eyebrow.

"On my honor, I would not give a young lady any encouragement to wait for me. How eligible young ladies weigh their options is thankfully not my problem. But what wise counsel do you have for me?"

"My only advice is this: I have never yet had a man ask me for advice regarding his intended. It is my general impression that men do not care to hear advice once their heart is set. As you are asking advice, I reason that your heart is not set."

"No. It isn't. But I cannot afford to be romantic, cousin."

"On the contrary. You cannot afford to marry without romance."

Darcy winced at the comment. "Is that so?"

"Yes. Your mother and father were said to have a great love for each other. Even our Aunt Catherine was very fond of her dear departed husband. So yes, you need a sensible woman to help you bear the burden of maintaining Pemberley, but for a truly happy life, do not lose sight of the prospect of love."

"You are right, cousin. Perhaps I am pressuring myself because Miss Bingley happens to be nearby. I will then not despair of finding love someday, somewhere."

"Good. I am glad to hear it. Now, forgive me, for I do not mean to sound like a mercenary, but as you know, I am not the eldest and like you, when I am introduced to a handsome woman of quality, I have my own interests at heart. By my observations of the past few days, am I correct in understanding that Miss Bingley has money?"

"Twenty thousand pounds," Darcy told him, cracking a wide smile. "I will not stand in your way if you would pursue Miss Bingley," Darcy continued. "Although I suspect gaining anything less than Pemberley through marriage will be a disappointment to her. It was written across her face from the moment she arrived here."

"Presently, my interest is limited to information gathering. As my humble personage cannot compete with the allure of Pemberley, I will be fighting a losing battle as long as you are without a spouse," Col. Fitzwilliam rightly noted. "But, if you were to find a wife who was not Miss Bingley, I could be there to console her, so to say. And be a constant connection to Pemberley as well."

"I do not intend to marry soon; it is not my wish that you, or

Miss Bingley, put your futures on hold for me. You may both be waiting for years."

"Miss Bingley adopts an expression of determination when she looks your way. I am not a foolish man nor interested in wasting my energy pursuing lost causes. For now, I will keep her on the periphery of my search for a spouse but do promise to write to me directly once you fall in love, dear cousin. Then I may circle back to Miss Bingley to woo her. But as for the idea of Miss Bingley becoming Mrs. Darcy, I have my doubts. There is a decided lack of possessiveness on your part in response to my interest in her."

Darcy smiled good-naturedly at his cousin's measured approach to securing his financial future and also to his ability to read Darcy's own heart. He clapped his cousin on the shoulder and strode into the orchard. The worries of the past few months seemed to evaporate in the presence of his trusted cousin and the diverting talk of matchmaking.

"So, our plans are set. I say, with Georgiana away, I will feel at odds rattling around Pemberley without her. I may take the party to London with me."

"Excellent plan."

"The orchard is abundant this year," Darcy observed. He plucked a ripe apple off a low-hanging branch, inhaled its warm fruity scent, and lobbed it unexpectedly to his cousin.

Col. Fitzwilliam's reflexes kicked in, and he caught the apple before it landed on the grass.

"Good one," Darcy laughed as he plucked a second apple for

himself and sunk his teeth into it.

# *CHAPTER FIVE*

"Georgiana, I need to speak with you," Fitzwilliam requested, standing in the doorway of her sitting room holding her everyday bonnet and parasol in his hand.

Georgiana put down her stitch work and looked up.

She smiled as she rose from her seat. "We are going outside?"

"Yes. Did I procure the right bonnet?" he asked. Georgiana's bonnets all looked the same to him, but he was not unconscious of the fact that, to ladies, there were very distinct differences.

"Indeed, you did," she replied as she tied the strings under her chin. They exited the house out of a side door and advanced down one of the more bucolic trails. Darcy waited until they were far from the house before beginning.

"Col. Fitzwilliam intends to make the journey to Rosings from here, and he has suggested that you accompany him and stay with your aunt and your cousin for several weeks. It is a fair proposition, and as we have not hired a new companion, the visit will allow us to put that decision off for the present."

"I would like to see my cousin," she replied. "I hope she is enjoying good health."

"As much as her mother will allow," Darcy quipped. "But if

you go, it will mean breaking off while the Bingley party is still here."

"I do not want to give offense," she hesitated.

"I will make your excuses. They will be made to understand that in a shared guardianship, I must yield to our cousin's influence."

"Thank you," she said.

"Unless you would not want to separate from anyone in the party for any other reason?" he hinted.

Sensing he meant Bingley, Georgiana replied diplomatically, "I look forward to seeing the Bingleys and Hursts when next in London but would not put off visiting Rosings at this time for their companionship."

Nodding, Darcy let the matter drop. He felt no disappointment in her lack of attachment to Bingley. As much as he desired the convenience of the match, he also wished to see his sister light up in the presence of her future husband. It was plain to see that Bingley ignited no such reaction in her. The matter was settled, and the next week saw Georgiana and Col. Fitzwilliam happily on their way to Rosings Park.

Caroline found it odd to hear that Georgiana was to be suddenly whisked off to Rosings with Col. Fitzwilliam when there had previously been no mention of the possibility. It appeared that Miss Darcy's summer was not organized ahead of time, as one would expect.

As Darcy did not confide in her, she was left to wonder and independently fill in the pieces of the story as well as she could. She had carefully listened in to their conversations once or twice, but she heard only muffled words and remained at a loss. In the flurry of activity that ensued with Georgiana's leave-taking, little thought was given as to what would happen next. She greatly desired to extend the stay at Pemberley, but with Georgiana safely at Rosings, she feared Darcy would become restless for new society.

However, her fears were unfounded, for as soon as the carriage carrying Georgiana and Col. Fitzwilliam disappeared around the bend, Darcy's spirits seemed suddenly lifted. He turned to his friends, who were gathered with him on the front drive to see the pair off, and said, "What do you think of keeping the party together and going to London?"

The Hursts, who had a home on Grosvenor Street, could easily decamp to London. Caroline would follow Darcy anywhere and Bingley, amiable as always, thought London would be wonderful, although he was always loathe to leave Pemberley when the weather was clement. But with promises to be invited back, Bingley and his family gladly exchanged the slow-paced days of the countryside for the stimulation of the city.

Darcy's invitation to prolong their connection surprised and pleased Caroline. She could not help but read into it—he was not ready to sever ties with her.

"It is one thing to form a friendship in the countryside, where close companionship is so necessary," Caroline whispered as she huddled with Mrs. Hurst in the privacy of her bedchamber that evening. "But to offer to take us to London! I cannot help but feel he has no reservations about being seen with me in smart society."

Mrs. Hurst, who was sensitive to her sister's aspirations, was quick to caution her. "From my observations, he does not care about society much. The only thing I am sure he cares about is his sister."

Caroline frowned. "I cannot agree. You have not studied him as I have. He sees me as a worthy companion. He is too well-mannered to single me out and compromise me before he is ready to declare a courtship, but mark my words, I believe I may leave Pemberley with little trepidation. My chances of returning permanently have greatly increased."

"I hope so. May I warn you to be circumspect in London. The ton will notice that you have set your cap for Darcy, and it is your reputation that will suffer if no engagement is forthcoming. At the least, do try to dance with strangers if asked."

"I am not worried about my reputation," Caroline insisted. "But I will dance, if asked, to please you."

***

The friends separated when in London, with Bingley accepting Darcy's invitation to stay with him.

"It will keep me from rattling around this big old place by myself," Darcy said. Caroline thought the move a smart one. Darcy had left instructions with his steward to forward news of new Derbyshire leases that came on the market as soon as possible. She trusted Darcy to persuade him in the right direction.

In the days that followed, they enjoyed all that London had to offer—private balls and dinners, promenading in the parks, and the best shopping. There was never a moment when Darcy tired of their company and with each passing week, Caroline Bingley felt even more deeply that Darcy should be hers.

"It cannot have escaped your attention how little interest he shows in any other young lady?" Caroline pointed out to Mrs. Hurst one Monday morning in September as she stood still while the seamstress pinned her hem.

"Perhaps you are right. Although he is no flirt like Charles, so I am not sure the comparison is just. Oh, I do like that silk."

"Yes, the perfect shade of blue. Just like Lady Darcy," she grinned.

"Ah … evoking pleasant memories on Darcy's part? Very clever," Mrs. Hurst replied.

"Marrying Darcy is serious business, Louisa. Anyway, I sincerely wish that Bingley and Miss Darcy would get on with it."

"That is a relationship that requires nurturing. On my part, I saw no mutual attraction between them. She thought only of her harp and he of horses and hunting while at Pemberley," Mrs. Hurst observed. "Hardly the behavior of two lovers. Try the ivory with that color."

The seamstress unspooled a length of ivory trim and held it up to the silk. Both sisters nodded their approval.

"And what of his foolish disregard of that beautiful Chipperton based only on its architectural style! An estate in Derbyshire could do so much for all of us. Well, me, particularly,"

Caroline complained.

They chuckled.

Caroline studied her look in the mirror. "Perfect. I believe I look the part already. Now, let us bring up the subject of Chipperton again at dinner. Bingley and Darcy are both expected tonight. With a little gentle prodding, we may convince him to give it a second look."

"Indeed. Where shall we go next?"

"There is a pearl comb I have my eye on at the jewelers," Caroline said. "The price is high, but I believe it is a necessary investment in my future. It will remind Darcy of someone he loved dearly."

However, their plans to persuade Bingley to reconsider Chipperton over dinner were scuttled when Darcy arrived at Grosvenor Street unaccompanied. That morning, Bingley had advised Darcy that he might be late and to go ahead without him. Caroline saw Bingley's late arrival as a stroke of luck that enabled her to speak frankly.

"You must convince Bingley of the rightness of Chipperton. This nonsense about the architecture is quite absurd," she urged him.

"It is a beautiful property," Darcy agreed. He swirled the whiskey in his glass. "I wonder at your brother's stubbornness as he is usually so agreeable."

"I might understand his reticence to purchase, but as it is only a lease he seeks, we must reason with him," Caroline stressed.

"Perhaps he needs to satisfy his curiosity by shopping around first?" Mr. Hurst suggested in Bingley's defense. "I looked at several properties before taking this one."

"True," Darcy said. "Having never had to lease a property, I can't imagine how one narrows down the choice. Disliking the look of a place seems as legitimate a reason as any other."

"Is there anything else in Derbyshire?" Caroline asked, her desperation leaking. "Bingley just loves it so."

Darcy shrugged his shoulders. "I trust in my steward to alert me if he hears of any news. Otherwise, changing Bingley's mind seems our best bet at this time."

"Agreed. Let us all work on him this evening when he arrives," Mrs. Hurst advised. "Let him question whether or not his refusal was rational, now that he has had time to think about it."

Dinner was called, and the party settled into the dining room. A quarter of an hour into the meal, Bingley's empty chair was remarked upon with growing curiosity.

"Wherever can he be? I'm so sorry he is not here," Caroline said to Darcy. "So unlike him to be late for dinner."

"He set out early this morning immediately after breakfast in a chaise and four saying he would be gone all day. True to his word, I have not seen him since," Darcy said.

"I suppose he'll show up sooner or later," Hurst chuckled. "Perhaps he had an assignation with a special young lady that he preferred to keep quiet?"

"Mr. Hurst, don't fantasize so!" Mrs. Hurst admonished her husband, taking a sidewise glance at Darcy.

"I know of no young lady in town with whom he would

venture to spend an entire day," Darcy added.

Caroline smiled across the table at Darcy and made a mental note to tell Mr. Hurst not to give the impression that Bingley had eyes for anyone other than Miss Darcy.

*My goodness, the conversations that had to be managed within one's own family,* Caroline thought with frustration.

"Mr. Hurst, your humor brightens our table considerably," Darcy said, "but I must agree with the ladies here. Bingley's whereabouts today are a puzzlement, even to me. He was unusually secretive about his destination, now that I reflect," Darcy added.

"He is most likely pulled into some card game at the club," Caroline mused. "The dangers of city life."

The main course was already underway when they heard doors slamming, followed by raised friendly voices and footsteps moving quickly throughout the house. Bingley burst into the room, trailing an air of excitement and apologizing profusely for his tardiness.

"Darcy, thank goodness you did not wait for me. I apologize for my lateness; it couldn't be helped."

"No apologies necessary, my good man," Mr. Hurst said.

"Welcome back," Caroline said with a motherly tone. "We've been wondering where you were."

Bingley smiled profusely at his companions as he sat down. He spread the large linen napkin wide across his lap and, with no small amount of drama, announced, "Well, I've done it!"

His statement temporarily stunned the party into silence, and for a moment, four blank faces stared back at him. Darcy, refusing to be baited into displaying any kind of curiosity, lifted his wine glass toward his friend and said dryly, "Congratulations, then, for whatever it is you've done."

"I dare say I am famished," Bingley exclaimed. "We stopped at a roadhouse halfway back but that feels like hours ago," he said, smiling roundly at his tablemates while the footman poured his wine and then hurried to his side with the serving platter.

"My goodness, Charles. Aren't you going to tell us what it is that you've done?" Caroline asked.

"Right," he said, picking up his fork and pausing to savor his news before announcing, "I leased an estate today. A glorious place called Netherfield Hall."

His news was met with disbelief.

"An estate? But how? Where?" Mrs. Hurst exclaimed.

Bingley took a swig of wine and nodded. "Isn't it a surprise? A marvelous surprise?"

Caroline swallowed and dabbed her lips with her napkin.

This was not the plan.

Not at all.

She struggled to maintain her composure.

"Netherfield Hall?" she repeated slowly. "Is it in Derbyshire?"

"No," he laughed.

"Is this a joke, Charles?" Caroline asked sharply.

"No, it's not a joke," he said happily. "A joke? Why? Why

should it be?"

"But we had not yet officially decided against Chipperton in Derbyshire," she said.

"Oh, we hadn't? How astonishing! I had quite forgotten about that place, which pales in comparison to Netherfield. I rode out to see it today with my man Andrews from the club, who tipped me off to it. Spent no more than a half-hour looking about the place, and even that was more than I needed as I loved it all, instantly, from the moment I laid eyes upon it."

Caroline felt her stomach churn. "And where is this Netherfield, may I dare to be informed?"

Bingley took a moment to chew his meat and take another sip of his wine. "Hertfordshire," he replied. "A most charming county. The house and park possess just the feel I was looking for. Its proprietor, a lovely fellow named Mr. Morris, had nothing but praise for the estate."

"Good job, man," Mr. Hurst replied. "Congratulations! I look forward to seeing it."

Mrs. Hurst shot her husband a look of horror and then addressed her brother. "You signed a lease?"

"Yes, I did."

"Oh, good heavens," Caroline exclaimed, resting her forehead in her hands.

"Why? Have I done something wrong?" he asked, sincerely bemused at his sisters' reactions.

"No, no, Bingley," Darcy soothed him. "If I'm reading the

situation correctly, you have merely shocked them. This is a decisiveness rarely seen in you. I am sure they are feeling the same and only need time to get used to the idea. But let me add my congratulations to those of Mr. Hurst."

"Thank you. Thank you very much," Bingley gushed. "I am quite enthusiastic."

"When do you plan to take up residence in this Netherfield Hall?" Mrs. Hurst asked. There was a marked disdain to her tone.

"At the end of the month," Bingley said. "There's a bit of work to be done beforehand—dusting and stocking the larder and getting the stables proper. But quick work, I expect. Then you must all come and stay."

"Splendid!" exclaimed Hurst, who was tiring of the smell of London.

"I see," Caroline said, refusing to add her congratulations to the men's. "Charles, I simply cannot share in this tumult of joy you are experiencing at the moment. I am aggrieved at not being part of the decision, particularly as I intend to keep house for you. I did so hope to tour the property with you beforehand. Was it necessary to be so rash?"

"It was a quick decision," Bingley admitted. "An impulse, so to say. You see, my friend Andrews has cousins who reside in the small town there—Meryton, it's called, and he tipped me off to the place. I dare say I am exceedingly grateful to Andrews and have nothing but good things to say about Meryton and its people as well. It is just the loveliest of places. It cast a spell on me."

"Good heavens! There and back in one day? What an obnoxiously long time on the road," Mrs. Hurst said with disgust.

"I know nothing of this Hertfordshire. Surely, it is not more beautiful than our intended Derbyshire? Did that county not cast a similar spell over your sensibilities?" Caroline asked.

"It is a different kind of beauty. A charm that is quite the best of England. I dare say, Caroline, you may fall in love with it yourself just as quickly as I did."

"I hardly think so." She looked down at her plate and smashed her peas, peeved at having no say in where her home was to be. She had been very clear in stating that she preferred Derbyshire only to have been completely ignored.

"Then let me offer a toast," Darcy said. "To Netherfield Hall!"

"To Netherfield Hall," the men exclaimed, raising their glasses. The women, however, were silent. Having lost her appetite, Caroline pushed back her chair and retired to her chambers immediately, not even bothering to proffer an excuse.

Despite hoping and praying that the leasing of Netherfield Hall was no more than a bad dream, Caroline's worst fears were realized when Bingley did not retract the lease. Shortly afterward, Bingley left for Hertfordshire, taking all of his belongings.

"I will write when it is ready for you all to come up," he said cheerily as he waved goodbye.

Caroline waved a half-hearted farewell to her brother and sat down in the Hursts' drawing room, dejected.

"I simply have no enthusiasm for this Hertfordshire. I know nothing about the neighborhood or its society," she said.

"I dare say it will pale in comparison to our dear Lambton," Mrs. Hurst sniffed.

Caroline sighed heavily. "So far from Pemberley! My only consolation in the matter is that Darcy has promised not to abandon us when it comes time to head there. See how he will not leave me?"

Mrs. Hurst nodded. "Darcy is faithful in his companionship. Surely we will not have to reside at this Netherfield for too long, as Georgiana will at some point quit Rosings, and Darcy will continue to require our company at Pemberley, for his sister's sake."

"Oh, to have a brother as thoughtful as Darcy! Instead, I am to be dragged around by my petticoats to some uncouth hinterlands. Hertfordshire? This is a bad business, Louisa. Bingley has always been impulsive, and now I am forced to suffer the effects of it in the dreariest of company." She waved her fan in front of her face and muttered with disgust, "Netherfield Park."

How she hated those two words already.

She sighed and sat quietly. With the back of her hand, she wiped her forehead. "It's warm today for autumn. I am anxious for a cool-down."

"The country air may be cooler," Mrs. Hurst ventured to guess.

Caroline rolled her eyes and shook her head dismissively. "Do not tease me so."

"Please do not despair," Mrs. Hurst urged her. "I promise

you, we will find a way out of this situation as we always have. I must confess, I am slightly curious to see what has captivated our brother so. And as for Bingley, remember, he has never stayed in one place for very long. I predict that this Netherfield Hall will be nothing but a passing fancy that we will laugh about later."

# *CHAPTER SIX*

There was no delight in Caroline's spirit when she received Bingley's letter setting the date for her move to Netherfield. Nor could she greet him with her usual portion of sisterly affection when he arrived in town to fetch them.

To make matters worse, Darcy delayed accompanying them to Netherfield as planned. He called on Grosvenor Street the afternoon before the move to deliver the news.

"I have been summoned to Rosings by my sister and cousin. Apparently, there is a new curate at Rosings. He is a great favorite of my aunt but a torrential bore who monopolizes their society. Georgiana and Fitzwilliam are desperate for me to join them as they say he has to be observed to be believed. As I can never refuse Georgiana anything she asks, off I must go. But I promise to come to Netherfield as soon as I can extricate myself from the family obligation."

"We will miss you," Bingley assured him. "I am sure time will fly by quickly and you will be at Netherfield in no time. I am anxious for you to see the place."

Caroline, drowning in her disappointment, could not contain her irritation and snapped, "I highly doubt time will fly in

Hertfordshire; don't be ridiculous. But do hurry, Darcy, and send our best wishes to your darling sister."

The Hursts echoed Caroline's true regret at the temporary loss of Darcy's companionship, which warmed Darcy's heart. Feeling he had let his friends down by the change of plans, he said, "Enjoy Hertfordshire. And, Miss Bingley, chin up. It is only a lease," he said, directing a rare smile her way.

The smile caused Caroline's heart to palpitate. Thus encouraged, she was better able to bear her fate.

***

"As I am not convinced this move will stick, I shall not haul all my belongings to Hertfordshire as Bingley has," Mrs. Hurst decided.

"That is good advice," Caroline said, nodding toward the new silk gown that was that day delivered from the seamstress. "My finer jewels and gowns would look out of place and the joy I derive from wearing them diminished."

With regret, Caroline left London. Their carriage neared Meryton late in the afternoon on a bright autumn day, and her stubborn opposition to the change was immediately softened by her first glimpse of the green, sunlit park stretching out before Netherfield Hall. Upon first approach, she could find little fault in the building itself, a well-proportioned two-story structure with a pleasing symmetry. Its front gate was flanked on either side by two grey stone columns, topped with impressive stone statues of reclining lions.

The carriage stopped before Netherfield's wide front steps, and Bingley proudly offered Caroline his arm as she disembarked, and he escorted her inside, a deference to her that she appreciated.

If Bingley was aware of his sister's reluctance, he did not show it, as his enthusiasm for Netherfield blinded him to all else. Yet, to his credit, Bingley had done well in directing the staff. Clean, polished floors and well-aired rooms helped ease Caroline's transition.

Caroline's sharp eye darted about the place as Bingley proudly led the party on its initial tour. She thought the furniture and hangings tolerable; some rooms were badly in need of an update—threadbare was the word that came to mind. Occasionally, Caroline's sharp eye would notice a crooked painting or a tilted candlestick, but in time, all that would be put to right. However, the large drawing rooms and dining areas, the rooms where she planned to sit each day, were nice enough, she decided. Overall, the rooms had a sturdiness that mirrored Pemberley, albeit on a much-reduced scale.

By the time she had finished drinking a restorative tea in its large drawing room, she no longer had quite the same issue with her brother's impulsiveness. She thought Netherfield was pretty enough to be tolerable until new plans could be forged.

"You simply must meet the neighbors. I have not met kinder people in all my travels," Bingley gushed as they sat together.

Caroline raised her eyebrows. "How nice for you. But I

would hesitate to call you well-traveled," she corrected him.

Bingley colored at her rebuke but was not dissuaded. "There is to be a local assembly tonight. We must all attend."

"Must we?" Mrs. Hurst whined. "I remain exceedingly sore from the journey." She adjusted a silk pillow at the small of her back.

"Dancing will renew your joints," Bingley insisted. "And I have already announced that you will all be in attendance. You must come. You must," Bingley pleaded, looking from face to face.

Hurst laughed. "Well, there it is. We cannot refuse. Your brother's reputation as a man of his word is on the line. We must go and do our best. I do believe we've endured worse company back home."

"That is true," Bingley acknowledged. "Our absence will give offense."

"Very well," Caroline gave in. "Exactly how far is it to whatever is the name of the place again?"

"It's Meryton. Meryton. And only two miles into town. Not far."

"I hardly know how to dress for such an event. Foolishly, I left my outdated dresses back home," Caroline complained.

"Resign yourself to being overdressed," Bingley said. "I, for one, never let my wardrobe affect my mood."

"But you are a man, Bingley! What kind of nonsense would that be when applied to a woman?" Mrs. Hurst shook her head and sighed in exasperation. "I'll wear my new lace then. And I assume any old dress will do."

***

Caroline found no comfort in being correct in her assumptions regarding the Meryton Assembly. It was hot, overcrowded, and utterly too boisterous for her tired nerves.

The evening dragged uncomfortably until the merciful moment when the music stopped and Bingley could be persuaded to leave his newfound friends and return home.

"What a splendid evening; I could have gone on for hours longer! How it inspires me to host my own ball. Netherfield needs music and light and dancing. Upon my honor, I believe Netherfield is just the place for dancing," he exclaimed in the privacy of their coach.

"Good heavens, dear brother. Take your time with these country folk; they are unknowns, and you have most likely already made yourself a prize to be plucked off," Caroline advised.

"Why do you think such thoughts? They are merely naturally friendly, that is all," Bingley attempted to convince her.

"You raised expectations by dancing twice with that pretty dark-haired one with the very pale complexion," Mrs. Hurst admonished him.

"Miss Bennet." Bingley smiled dreamily. "I did admire her so. Her father was neighborly enough to call on me earlier, and I quite enjoyed the visit. We talked about his library."

"Miss Bennet is her name? I dare say she was the only exceptional young lady in the mob," Caroline decreed.

"She seemed cheerful enough, despite her obviously low rank. We are not talking about lords and ladies here," Mrs. Hurst snickered.

"Her father is a gentleman and that makes her worthy of my notice. Let us call on her soon," Bingley suggested with enthusiasm.

"I would not object fully to a further acquaintance, as Louisa and I cannot isolate ourselves from all the local young women," Caroline replied slowly, with a slight tone of contempt for the society she unwillingly found herself in. "I may go so far as to invite her to dine once we are settled."

"That would be marvelous," Bingley enthused.

"Don't hold your breath. I said *may*," Caroline clarified, signaling the end of the conversation by turning her head toward the window and fixing her gaze outside.

Bingley fell silent, his excitement dampened by the general low mood of his companions.

"You must be careful of the eager young ladies. You were quite the talk of the evening," Hurst drawled from across the coach.

"Was I?" Bingley asked happily.

"I noted little beauty or fashion in this assemblage. I took no pleasure from it," Mrs. Hurst stated matter-of-factly.

"I so disagree!" Bingley exclaimed. "Miss Bennet is a diamond, and I thought her sisters very pretty as well."

"It was a strain to be in a large room of complete strangers. I consider myself naturally cheerful, but even my cheeks hurt from forcing a smile. I will probably be thought rude for giving up by the evening's end," Caroline said.

"I'm sure you made a good enough effort for this sort," Mrs. Hurst said, stifling a yawn.

"Oh, thank goodness we are home," Caroline exclaimed as the lit windows of Netherfield Hall appeared in the distance. The words escaped her lips involuntarily—she had not meant to call Netherfield Hall her home.

***

A week later, the Bennet girls called at Netherfield to welcome their new neighbors. They stayed for an hour, drinking coffee and making quick work of the iced buns, just like the ones served at Pemberley, which Bingley insisted be served.

It was a large group—the five Bennets, plus Bingley and his sisters and Mr. Hurst. Bingley was delighted to play the host, but his heroic attempts to pay equal attention to all five sisters failed, as he could not help but focus primarily on the eldest, Miss Jane Bennet. Occasionally, he remembered his manners and directed a comment about the weather or a question about the neighborhood to one of her sisters. Despite his genuine desire to remain impartial, he soon grew impatient waiting out the answer and went back to focusing on Miss Bennet.

Caroline found the present company to be not very interesting and their manners and day wear not at all fashionable. The second eldest, Elizabeth, seemed always to be glancing about the room with a look of comic observation, which irked Caroline.

After the call ended and the room was private, Caroline remarked, "Who is Miss Elizabeth to look so impertinently about the room? Did you notice, Bingley?"

"Did I notice?" he asked with indifference. "No. I do not know what you are talking about."

In truth, Bingley had noticed Elizabeth but not for the same reason his sister had. Instead, he thought Elizabeth's quick wit and playful countenance stood out amongst the sisters. He had no memory of Elizabeth from the assembly. In fact, his mind was only now beginning to have some success in pairing the new names and faces and then organizing them into the local Meryton families.

But at Netherfield, he found Miss Elizabeth to be a lively presence that effortlessly kept the conversation going. He was almost as impressed with Miss Elizabeth's charm and intelligence as he was with Miss Jane's beauty.

Bingley was desperately sorry to see all the sisters go, so intently did he enjoy having such a large number of young women come to call. That sentiment, however, was not shared by either of his sisters.

"It was obvious to me that the Bennets were more interested in bringing back a report on the inside of Netherfield than they were in deepening the acquaintance," Caroline said. "How they would sneakily look around at everything when they thought I wasn't watching. But, of course, *they* would be curious as to the accommodations of folks above them." She nodded her head in unconscious agreement with herself.

"And what appetites these young ladies displayed! I thought two dozen buns would be an excessive amount but look, we have but a scant amount leftover," Mrs. Hurst observed, reaching for the tray to take a third iced bun for herself and another for her husband.

Bingley perked up at the mention of the iced buns. "Did you enjoy them? I know they can't compare to those served at Pemberley, but were they close enough, do you think?"

"Yes, good enough, more than good enough for this lot," Hurst said, licking his fingers. "Just like at Pemberley."

The door opened, and the housemaids entered to stoke the fire and light the lamps as dusk was upon them.

"Thank you, Miss Lilly, Miss Hanna," Caroline said, watching them with a steady eye as they went about their tasks somewhat more clumsily than Caroline wished to see.

"Speaking of Pemberley, I have had a letter from Darcy. He arrives in a fortnight," Bingley announced.

"Oh, thank heavens!" Caroline exclaimed, reluctantly turning her attention away from the staff. "It has been so tedious without him."

"Did you warn him?" Hurst said with a twinkle in his eye.

"Warn him about what?" Bingley asked, genuinely confused.

"That he's walking into the frying pan," Hurst chuckled. "If those young ladies who just called on us find out about Darcy's wealth, he will never get a moment's peace here. They will be on him like flies."

Caroline smirked. "That is a very funny conjecture, Mr. Hurst. Darcy has always been sought after. Be assured that his natural aloofness will send the appropriate message to all the locals and their mothers. But I imagine we will all have a good laugh watching the Bennet girls fall all over him, trying to outdo each other with flattery. I am quite looking forward to watching such predictable comedy."

"Let me join in the fun by suggesting that you must also warn him about Netherfield," Mrs. Hurst said with a coy smile.

"How so?" Bingley asked innocently, furrowing his brow as he actively tried to recall some flaw in the place so treacherous that he owed Darcy a precautionary warning.

"Why, that it is no Pemberley! He will think you have found an equal in its size and grace. As his good friend, you should warn him to temper his expectation so that at first glance he will not think himself directed to the wrong address." Mrs. Hurst howled at her remarks, and Caroline did not care to hold back her mirth either.

Bingley did not mind and laughed as well.

He felt he could afford to laugh at himself occasionally. He was most pleased with his current life and felt convinced that Darcy would see the wisdom in his choice and applaud his taste.

"Oh, heavens," he suddenly shouted out, and with a look of sheer panic about his face, he rushed over to the hearth and began furtively stomping his boot on the carpet as the odor of burning wool wafted through the room. With a fast action, he rolled a small errant log back onto the hearth.

So fast were Bingley's reflexes that the incident was safely handled before the room's occupants could react.

"Luckily, I happened to be watching, and I saw it roll out," Bingley explained.

"Who was working the fire?" Caroline asked. "Was it Miss Lilly?"

"Yes, it was her," said Mrs. Hurst. "I noticed beforehand that she is sloppy. A crooked tablecloth here, drips and dribbles of tea spilled there." She tut-tutted and shook her head.

"She is young and green and moves too fast. I will have a word with her about this," Caroline said firmly. "Carelessness in setting a fire is dangerous."

"I imagine it is difficult finding quality staff so far out here in Hertfordshire," Mr. Hurst commented. "Miss Lilly wouldn't last two days in London's finer homes." He walked over to the window and lifted the sash, waving away the odor of the burnt carpet with his hands.

"That's not true," Bingley protested, suddenly protective of his hire. "I say, accidents can happen anywhere."

"I suppose you are right, Bingley," Caroline said. "But as the mistress of the house, it falls to me to reprimand her so that such accidents are reduced to rare occasions. Now, what were we talking about?"

"Darcy's arrival. I dare say he will love this place. He will understand why I admire it so. And to show it off, I have made up my mind to host a ball. It is the best way to welcome all my friends and family to Meryton. By golly, it will be a splendid means to introduce him to all our neighbors. Now that's something to look forward to."

Caroline rolled her eyes. "Goodness, Bingley! You are more likely to scare him off with this mangy lot."

"He famously won't dance with strangers, so why bother? If you want a ball, don't wait for Darcy," Hurst huffed. "Throw it now."

But Bingley was enamored with the idea of waiting for Darcy. Over the next few weeks, at private dinners or at the shops, he talked of nothing but his desire to throw a ball, teasing the locals that it would be a night to remember until his sisters told him to either set a date or be quiet.

He consulted his calendar and determined that the moon would be perfect the night that Darcy arrived, and so the date was set. Thus decided, he spent the entirety of the next day riding about, inviting the whole neighborhood. At dinner that evening, he again raved about Miss Bennet, who had been at home when he delivered the invitation. Purposely, he had saved the Bennet residence for last and was rewarded by being invited to stay for tea.

"Miss Elizabeth suggested that we might join her and her party tomorrow on a walk to a place called Oakham Mount, should the weather be clement. We could take the coach to the meeting point and hike up the hill from there. Would anyone care to join me?"

"I may go, but I expect this walk to be as unimpressive as the shops here in Meryton," Caroline complained.

“How I miss shopping in Lambton with Miss Darcy,” Mrs. Hurst said. “But I will go with you tomorrow, for lack of something better to do.” Having sat at home the past few days, they had run out of ways to pass the time. The prospect of a group activity cheered them.

# *CHAPTER SEVEN*

Abundant sunshine and moderate temperatures greeted them the next day, and the excursion to Oakham Mount was underway. Upon arriving at the pre-ordained meeting point, Caroline was surprised to see that a large party awaited. Most of the Bennet sisters appeared to be present, and she recognized Charlotte Lucas and her sister, and another young lady who was introduced as Miss Mary King.

The hike commenced, and Bingley immediately attached himself to Miss Jane and walked briskly ahead with her and Miss Elizabeth. Ever observant, Caroline noticed Miss Maria Lucas and Miss Mary King roll their eyes at the pairing off.

"How surprising," Miss Maria said drolly.

"Should I even bother to attend his ball knowing that he only cares about Miss Jane and no one else?" asked Miss King.

"I shouldn't stay back if I were you. Perhaps he has friends that may also be at the ball, and we might stand a chance with them?" Maria guessed.

Charlotte, who was with the two young women, shushed them.

"Please be quiet. They will overhear you."

Caroline and Mrs. Hurst exchanged glances but said nothing. Charlotte, who was walking immediately ahead, glanced behind her and then excused herself to fall back and keep company with Caroline and Mrs. Hurst.

"I hear this is your first time at Oakham. The colors are particularly pretty this autumn," Charlotte said. "We try to take the hike at least once every fall."

Caroline appreciated Charlotte's swift redirection of the conversation away from the young ladies' most interesting complaints about Bingley's attentions to Miss Jane. It showed an awareness that Caroline appreciated, and thus she willingly played along.

"The scenery is quite delightful," Caroline said simply, while Mrs. Hurst murmured similar sentiments.

The trio walked along, admiring the trees, the incline, and the sky, while all along Caroline kept her gaze focused on Bingley up ahead, who chattered on in happy oblivion to the criticism brewing behind his back. Miss Lucas was an easy conversationalist, and neither woman minded the other's company, so they enjoyed a very pleasant hike up the mountain.

Charlotte, to Caroline's delight, seemed to speak very freely about her neighbors, and eventually, Caroline led the conversation around to Miss Jane.

"Miss Jane and my brother seem to be fast friends," Caroline observed. "She is so pretty that I am surprised she is not already married at … how old is she? Forgive me for prying, but Bingley is terrible with details."

"It is perfectly reasonable to be naturally curious about a young lady when your brother seems attached," Charlotte answered. "Miss Jane is two and twenty."

"And besides her, there are four unwed sisters," Mrs. Hurst said. "How unfortunate."

"And an entail, which makes it so much worse." Charlotte shook her head.

"An entail?" Caroline asked. "To whom?"

"I believe to a distant cousin of Mr. Bennet's. My mother says Mrs. Bennet worries so about being thrown out before her daughters have made advantageous matches."

"One cannot blame her," agreed Mrs. Hurst. Caroline fell silent, considering how Jane's marriage to Bingley would change the Bennet family's fortunes and ruin her own life at the same time.

While Jane herself might be a perfectly pleasant young lady and easy to manipulate, her family's lack of rank, horrendous manners, and financial desperation posed a host of problems. Caroline envisioned a constant parade of Bennet women coming in and out of Netherfield.

"Bingley is quite fickle," Caroline said purposely. "He falls in love almost everywhere we go. We are quite used to these passing fancies on his part."

"Does he?" Charlotte said, with an air of surprise in her tone.

Caroline laughed inwardly. She knew this bit of information would be passed around Meryton quickly, as was her intent.

"Yes," Mrs. Hurst piped in. "Why, he was just attached to

two women in Bath this very summer before we moved onto Derbyshire."

"How very interesting," Charlotte said, twisting her mouth in disapproval.

They had reached the top of the mount and joined the others there. They enjoyed a quick, light picnic while their feet and legs rested in the sunshine.

To his credit, Bingley did manage to tear himself away from Miss Jane to participate in the group conversation. Still, the day's events convinced the sisters that Bingley's behavior, and his enthusiasms, needed checking.

As soon as they were back in the comfort of their drawing room, seated before the late afternoon fire, Caroline said, "What a delightful walk we had with Miss Lucas."

"Now there is a sensible young woman with a very fine family," Mrs. Hurst added.

"Yes, indeed. Miss Lucas is a very nice young lady," Bingley agreed.

"You might spend some of your time talking to her, instead of Miss Jane, the next time we all gather together," Caroline advised. "You run no risk of losing Miss Jane's attentions, as she does not appear to have any other prospects. Nor does she seem as enthralled by the regiment as her sisters, so you may take your time. Perhaps you might explore if there are other young ladies in town who might make suitable companions for you."

"Why do you advise me so? Can I not make my own choices?

Do you dislike Miss Jane?" he said, with some distress in his tone.

"Her lineage is unimpressive; compare hers to say, Miss Darcy's," said Mrs. Hurst.

"And there is another disturbing bit of news that we are obliged to disclose to you," Caroline added.

"Disturbing?" Bingley put down his teacup and saucer in preparation of bad news. "Is Miss Jane betrothed to another?"

"No, no, do not jump to such dramatic conclusions, Bingley. I simply was told in passing that there is an entail on Longbourn, which would make the Bennet women more desperate than the average family lucky enough to have sons."

"An entail?" Bingley repeated. "That is a bad thing for Miss Jane?"

"It could be," Mrs. Hurst said. "If anything happened to Mr. Bennet then his distant cousin, who is set to inherit, could put out Mrs. Bennet and any unmarried daughters, or so I've been told."

"Oh dear, I do hope nothing happens to Mr. Bennet," Bingley said worryingly. "He seems healthy enough and from what I have observed, seems to drink and eat in moderation."

"Yes, yes, he is perfectly fine currently, and we are not saying anything will happen to him, mind you," Caroline clarified. "But should Miss Jane marry a wealthy man who lived but three miles down the road, well, that would provide a certain level of security for her future that the elder Mrs. Bennet does not now possess. It would be a powerful motivation to pressure her pretty eldest daughter into a courtship with you, no matter what Miss Bennet's true feelings be.

Goodness, we are newcomers in Meryton, and Jane has lived her entire life here. She may already be in love with a stable boy or a poor local farmer but be required by her mother to hold out for an advantageous match."

Bingley suddenly appeared strained and tired. Sensing his dismay, Caroline sought to reassure him of her good intentions. "I am only telling you so that you are aware of the scenario and do not feel uninformed. I know how much you appreciate information," Caroline flattered him.

"It is right for you to do so. You are always so sensible, Caroline," Bingley agreed warily.

Caroline smiled. Bingley was always so tragically susceptible to suggestion.

"Caroline is only trying to help you," Mrs. Hurst said to Bingley. "You should thank her for always having your best interests at heart."

"Yes, you are correct. Thank you, Caroline, for the information. I, I, promise to …" he stammered and looked lost, not knowing quite what to say.

"To take your time to get to know Miss Bennet before assuming you are in love with her?" Caroline offered.

Bingley nodded. "Yes, to take my time to get to know Miss Bennet. But I've already agreed that I would call on her tomorrow. I don't want to back out on my word."

"No one is asking that. But taking your time to get to know her is a very wise decision," Caroline said. "I'm sure you won't regret it. If in, say, six or eight months, you still feel that Miss Jane is the best young lady of your acquaintance, and she is still unattached and returns your favor, then you will have no reason to doubt her affections the way you might if you act rashly and give her everything she wants too quickly."

Bingley nodded and sighed deeply. He picked up his teacup and took a sip. The tea was too cool for his preference, and so he put it down and silently gazed out the window, feeling very let down by the afternoon's discussion.

***

The next day, with Caroline's permission, all except Mr. Hurst paid a call at Longbourn, where they were heartily welcomed. The Bingley sisters had never been and, as expected, were underwhelmed by the residence.

The conversation revolved around the upcoming ball until Bingley happened to mention Darcy's anticipated inclusion. Almost immediately, the conversation pivoted, filled with veiled attempts by Mrs. Bennet to discover more details about Mr. Bingley's friend.

To Mrs. Bennet's frustration, all Bingley would say was that his friend was a delightful fellow, and he guaranteed they would all feel the same as soon as they met him. He was careful not to incite anticipation about Darcy in Jane. Both Caroline and Mrs. Hurst thought privately that the Bennet girls were so below Darcy's notice that there was no need for Bingley to bother being circumspect about

Darcy's position or wealth. Nevertheless, they too refrained from saying anything outright about his station or Pemberley.

The call at Longbourn passed quickly enough, although Bingley would have stayed all day. After an hour in Jane's company, he felt as if he were dancing on air but did not want his sisters surveying his mood and then reminding him of the previous day's conversation regarding caution. Knowing that the carriage ride back home to Netherfield would be filled with his sisters' critical observations on Longbourn, he chose to walk home in order to protect his heightened spirits.

Naturally, this left his sisters the perfect opportunity to render their exacting critique of Longbourn.

"I dare say it is genteel enough but decidedly cramped for so many people," Mrs. Hurst said with a slight shudder at the idea of having to share a chamber with one or the other of the sisters.

"The structure is quaint enough in its own way. The real problem with Longbourn is that it houses Mrs. Bennet. What a tragedy for these young women to have such a mother," Caroline said. "Men of quality will avoid the connection; I can assure you."

"Most young men in the throes of passion do not care one bit about their mother-in-law, no matter how appalling," Mrs. Hurst said.

"Men of class will," Caroline replied, thinking of Darcy.

"I disagree most heartily."

"I am right. You will see," Caroline said, patting her sister on the knee reassuringly.

Both sisters agreed that having exchanged calls, there was little need of putting themselves out any further with the Bennet family. "Our next call should be to Lady Lucas. I am most curious to hear how they came to be titled," Mrs. Hurst said.

"Let us bring Bingley with us and watch as Lady Lucas throws her daughters in his way," Caroline suggested. "At the least, it will keep him from making yet another call at Longbourn."

"What an amusing idea. I dare say, we should parade our brother before all the young women and mothers of Meryton before the ball. We can keep him so busy that he will not have time for Miss Jane. And just think of the angst it will incur in a certain Mrs. Bennet when she hears that Bingley is bestowing his company on all the young women in town and not just her eldest daughter."

"That will serve her right," Caroline said. "I like this idea, Louisa. I like it very much. Leave it to me to handle it with our brother."

# *CHAPTER EIGHT*

The combination of the approaching ball and the arrival of Fitzwilliam Darcy soon threw the Netherfield household into a frenzy of activity. The nicest guest chamber was aired and laid out with new linens, great batches of white soup stirred up, and special care taken to provide for all of Darcy's preferences, including his favorite cigars and whiskeys ordered from London.

"I want Netherfield to be as much a haven to Darcy as Pemberley was to me," Bingley confided in Caroline.

"Good luck with that. Instead of trying to convince Darcy that Netherfield is in the same league as Pemberley, why not just aim to have a pleasant fortnight or two together?"

This sisterly advice made much sense to Bingley.

"But what concerns me more, Bingley," Caroline went on to say, "is the ball. I am concerned about the perceived slights I fear may have already occurred amongst your other invited guests."

"Perceived slights? What do you mean?" Bingley's expression was one of confusion.

Caroline demurred, pretending to weigh her words.

"It has come to my attention, and I am honor-bound not to reveal how, that other families have noticed your favoritism to the

Bennet women. Suffice it to say that, for your ball to be the success I know you desire it to be, then you must do some necessary repair work in the neighborhood beforehand."

Bingley was troubled at the news. Caroline snuck a look at him and was encouraged to see genuine regret etched on his face.

"I meant no offense. I mean, I admit I have seen the Bennets more lately than other families, but how did the others … I mean, I wonder how you know? Did someone say something?"

"How do your neighbors know about your favoritism toward the Bennets?" Caroline led him on soothingly. "Why, my poor dim brother, idle young ladies have nothing to do but gossip."

"Oh, I see," Bingley said, coloring. "Have I put a foot wrong?"

Caroline shook her head in sympathy. "I am afraid so, but I beg you, do not berate yourself. You are unfamiliar with the ways of small-town gossip and simply made a misjudgment. If you were not intent on hosting this ball, I would hardly press you on the issue, but since there is already a river of some discontent flowing in the neighborhood, I must urge you to make amends as soon as possible. Otherwise, I am afraid some families are already talking about staying back from the ball."

"No! Say it is not so! Tell me, what should I do to make appropriate amends?" Bingley was crestfallen to think of himself as having caused pain to the villagers that had uniformly welcomed him with open arms.

"I can hardly suggest that I know the best way to ease their hurt feelings. But why don't we do this? Let us call on as many families as we can before the ball. I imagine an hour or two of concentrated attention will assuage any existing feelings of neglect or favoritism toward the Bennets."

"Yes, let us do that. I have been remiss in paying my calls to my new friends. Can we start tomorrow? Oh dear, can we get it done in time?"

"I am certain we can if we put our minds to it. Tomorrow we call on Lady Lucas. Why don't we start there?"

Bingley agreed.

"Let us pay our visits, one by one. Show interest in their lives, and I guarantee you they will not hold a grudge against you. But, to truly rectify the situation, I am afraid there is one more detail."

"Yes, what is it?"

"You must refrain from visiting the Bennets again before the ball. Otherwise, you may appear to be insincere in your amends."

"Of course. You are right."

"After the ball you can be as indiscriminate as you like with the Bennets."

"Yes, yes, I believe you are right. Thank you, Caroline, for your wise counsel."

"Do not mention it," Caroline smiled back. "But make me proud tomorrow. Even if you have no intention of engaging the hearts of these local women, making them feel as if you might at some point will make your ball a smashing success, and the talk of the town."

Bingley wanted that very much, and so he and his sisters began his tour of the Meryton homes the next day, with the aforementioned call to Sir William Lucas and his wife and daughters. In little over an hour, Bingley was so complimentary of the room and the hospitality, so interested in the minute details of their lives, and so attentive to the daughters that even the very humble Charlotte noticed the change in his manner.

Despite previously thinking he was all in for Jane Bennet, after Bingley's visit, she was not so certain. Sir William was so pleased with the call that the next week he sent over a dozen young saplings to be planted in the Netherfield lawn.

Then it was on to the Kings; Mary King was left feeling hopeful of Bingley's affections, and her mother sent over a dozen eggs in gratitude.

Over the next fortnight, Bingley dutifully called on all the other invited Annes and Mariannes and Doretheas and Katherines and Harriets and Margarets of Meryton. In an earnest effort to dispel the charge of favoritism, he displayed genuine interest in the health and well-being of all his future guests. The majority of these young women and their mothers wildly misinterpreted his attention, and the embers of hope were enflamed in their hearts. Breads and sweets, flowers and potted plants began arriving for Bingley from many households, right up until the ball.

Caroline thought it all terribly amusing. "Poor Bingley. There is only one of him, and that will not be enough to satisfy this gaggle of hopefuls and their mothers," she giggled, unwrapping a taffy from a box sent that day.

"Poor Miss Bennet. She will find herself competing for Bingley in a way she is unaccustomed," Mrs. Hurst laughed, her mouth full of sweets. "Whoever thought that life in the countryside could be so entertaining?"

***

Darcy's letter said he would arrive the morning of the ball. As was typical, the list of last-minute tasks that would require Bingley's attention grew, but the imminent arrival of his good friend left him too distracted to concentrate. He swiftly passed all the duties off to his sisters in exchange for pacing the front steps of Netherfield in anticipation of Darcy's coach.

Caroline and Mrs. Hurst applied their no-nonsense approach to household management, and a sense of order and control settled upon the place. The only trouble came at the hands of Miss Lilly, who being a bundle of nerves and excitement, sadly lost her grip on a vase of flowers meant for the entry hall. It came crashing down, scattering water, stems, petals, and shards of glass across the floor.

"Oh, Miss Bingley, my apologies," she cried out, her face contorted in angst.

Caroline held her tongue. The vase was nothing of value, and she prided herself on being a generous but firm employer. A teaching opportunity was now before her.

"Tears are not necessary, Miss Lilly. The vase held little value.

I am more concerned about the inconvenience and mess as Mr. Darcy is due imminently, so we must make haste in the clean up. But may I take this opportunity to advise you to move more slowly when engaged in your duties? There is no race to the finish in this household. Instead, I advise you to move slowly and graciously, as if you were confident in your abilities. If I can see improvement in you in this area, then that will more than make up for this mistake."

Miss Lilly wiped the tears streaming down her red splotchy cheeks with the back of her hand and made a clumsy curtsy. "Thank you, Miss Bingley," she said. "It won't happen again."

"You are more than welcome," Caroline replied. "Now get the broom and the pan; time is of the essence." Miss Lilly hurried off, but while she was fetching the broom, Caroline saw Darcy's coach emerge from the cover of the trees.

"Oh, my goodness," Mrs. Hurst exclaimed as she entered the hall. "What happened?

"Careful where you step," Caroline warned. "There's glass everywhere and now Darcy is here."

"Who did it?"

Caroline rolled her eyes. "Do I have to say?"

"Miss Lilly?" Mrs. Hurst guessed as Caroline confirmed with a nod. Mrs. Hurst laughed merrily.

"She is off getting the broom, but Darcy will have to go around the side entrance," Caroline decided. "There is too much mess."

At the sight of Darcy's coach, Bingley rushed down the front stairs to greet his friend. Both men were pleased to be reunited, and Darcy was in an especially good humor. His visit to Rosings had assured him that Georgiana was thriving in the company of their relatives. Feeling that his world was in order, Darcy was relaxed and at ease.

Bingley led Darcy to the front steps, but Caroline opened the door.

"Mr. Darcy, welcome to Netherfield," she said cheerily.

He tipped his hat and returned the greeting.

Bingley, eager to commence showing off Netherfield, waited for his sister to clear the door, but she remained put.

"I am afraid the hall is inaccessible at the moment. I apologize," she said, looking at Darcy. He was just as attractive as ever. His pale complexion seemed to highlight his fine features and provided a stark contrast with his dark hair and eyes. She perceived his eyes to be twinkling at the sight of her.

"What do you mean?" Bingley asked.

She held out her hand to halt his progress. She slowly opened the door, revealing the pool of water and strewn stems.

"I am afraid there is glass everywhere. It is not safe to walk on until cleaned up." She smiled and said specifically to Darcy, "The staff we have available here in Hertfordshire is hopeless. I'm afraid that Netherfield is far from running like clockwork."

Mr. Darcy smiled at the scene and said, "Do not fret. We have the occasional smash-up at Pemberley as well."

"Very well, we'll go around the side door. I'm so sorry about the inconvenience; it is not the grand entrance I anticipated, my friend," Bingley said. He and Darcy bounded back down the steps and around to the side entrance.

Once safely inside Netherfield, Darcy was complimentary in his assessment.

"A generous park, situated on a nice rise with a commanding prospect and good-sized rooms with cross ventilation," Darcy enthused. He clapped Bingley on the back. "Well done, my friend."

After enduring his sisters' sour reactions to Netherfield, Darcy's approval meant much to Bingley. "I'm so glad you approve," Bingley gushed. "Now wait until tonight, when you meet the locals," he added, and he blushed uncharacteristically, which Darcy was quick to pick up.

"Any local in specific I should be aware of?" Darcy teased, arching his brow.

"Yes, there is one lady I'm quite agog over," Bingley confessed, turning redder.

"Be sure to point her out then as soon as you are able. I am quite fatigued from the journey and may make an early exit from the night. Please forgive me in advance," Darcy warned.

As Bingley would never impose unduly on his good friend, he readily excused Darcy from any obligation of the evening beyond requesting a few compulsory dances with his sisters. "They did miss your company so," Bingley added.

"How kind you are to say that," Darcy responded. "And of course, yes to the dances."

The remainder of the day passed quickly, and the start of the ball was soon upon them. Caroline's idea to parade Bingley from home to home did its job; carriage after carriage of hopeful young women drove down the lane to Netherfield that moonlit night, each convinced it would soon be hers.

***

News of Bingley's gallivanting about the neighborhood had reached Jane Bennet, but her heart was so humble that she immediately scolded herself for the small pangs of jealousy that plagued her.

Jane tried not to feel slighted when Bingley selected Charlotte Lucas as his partner to begin the ball, although Elizabeth felt the pain for her. Bingley seemed to put Jane off on purpose, and both Jane and Elizabeth began to suspect that the night would end in humiliation. Two, three, four more dances passed, and still Bingley did not choose Jane for his partner.

Eventually, Bingley did approach Jane for a dance, and as he took her hand, he said in a low voice so that only she could hear, "I have saved the best for last." He gave her hand an affectionate squeeze, causing Jane's heart to overflow with joyful sentiments.

From across the room, Mrs. Bennet observed Jane and Bingley with a sense of triumph. Mr. Darcy, hovering on the outskirts of the dance, saw the difference in Bingley as he watched the pair go up and down the line together. Bingley was lost in Jane's eyes, oblivious to the watching gaze of the guests.

Caroline, too, saw the delight on Bingley's face.

She sighed and looked away.

Bingley was hopeless.

Instead, she comforted herself with thoughts of Fitzwilliam Darcy. His attentions to her that night had dramatically shifted her hopes. She reflected on how Darcy had approached her for the first dance, doing nothing more than holding out his hand to her. They were already communicating on a level that required no words. She convinced herself that she would soon be concerned with bigger, more significant matters than her brother's future. As the mistress of Pemberley, the goings-on at Netherfield would be beyond her notice.

In fact, Darcy's presence was a topic of some conversation at the ball. Despite Bingley's previous reticence to describe Darcy as a man of wealth, the truth of his superior consequence was soon common knowledge among the locals. This information was delivered via the loose lips of Mr. Hurst, who saw no good reason to refrain from speaking about money. Finding little in common with the guests and having imbibed the spiced punch generously since twilight, he fell to talking about Darcy. He described Darcy's income, his properties in Derbyshire and London, and even his livestock and carriages with great detail and equal embellishment.

As word of Darcy's wealth circulated, all the village matrons found their way to Hurst, eager to hear the details firsthand. Thus, the mothers of Meryton, who were so let down earlier in the evening by Bingley's clear preference for Jane, were suddenly distracted by the prospect of engaging the affections of the very eligible Mr. Darcy. By the end of the evening, all talk was of Darcy, and the consensus was that in looks, manner, and property, such a man was not often seen in their local society.

When had he arrived?

How long was he to stay?

And most importantly, was he looking for a wife?

Mr. Darcy could not avoid hearing his income whispered about. Nor was he oblivious to the hungry glances of the mothers aimed his way. His desire to remove himself from the evening and seek solace in the privacy of his chamber greatly increased. The locals, though boisterous and harmless, possessed nothing to tempt him on a day he had traveled. He patiently waited out the hour or two of attendance his manners required of him.

He kept moving, stopping at the refreshment table then walking onto the deserted side terrace to take the air then back through some of the less populated corridors and rooms, looking very much like he was on his way to somewhere pressing.

He forced himself to return to the crowd in order to pull Bingley aside and tell him he was retiring when he realized the assembled musicians had stopped and that the chatter had died. He stopped very close to the assembly, not eager to make a grand entrance into a quiet room when the most beautiful, bird-like trill filled the air. A woman was singing.

Her voice was clear and confident and so sweet that, for the first time that evening, his interest was piqued. Who was the lucky woman to possess such a pure, angelic voice? He walked slowly into the room, slipping in unnoticed, as all eyes were rapt upon the vocalist. She sang without artifice or pride, and whilst she did not usurp Miss Jane Bennet in beauty there was a charm in her presence that quite enchanted Darcy. He leaned his broad shoulders against the wall and time seemed to stand still.

And when the song ended, he felt a peculiar expectation that she should sing again, but the young lady rose from the bench to give way to another. Not wishing to prolong his evening any further, he slipped out of the room as silently as he had slipped in and made his way up to his room. He decided that a personal good night to Bingley was not only unnecessary but would ruin the mood of the moment.

He fell asleep and dreamt of songbirds.

# *CHAPTER NINE*

Darcy kept the memory of the intriguing singer to himself while the movements of the ball were thoroughly discussed the next day. There seemed to be somewhat of an upset in the household resulting from Bingley's continuing favoritism of Miss Bennet.

"It was not lost how you lit up in the company of Miss Jane. It was commented on frequently last night despite all of our efforts beforehand," Caroline complained.

"When I go to town next, I expect to hear engagement rumors, courtesy of Mrs. Bennet," Mrs. Hurst teased him.

Bingley looked his sister squarely in the eye. "The rumors would be true, then," he announced.

"Charles, don't tease me so. This is serious," Caroline said.

"It is you who do not understand me," Bingley declared. "For I have written to Mr. Bennet today and asked for a half-hour of his time. I plan to ask for his permission to pursue his daughter in a courtship that I hope will end in marriage. I am sorry if this does not cause you joy. I am over the moon."

"Bingley, is this true?" Darcy asked.

"Yes, it is," Bingley nodded.

"Has your request for an audience been granted?" Caroline

inquired. Her immediate reaction was to start estimating the amount of time needed to gather everyone's things in a trunk and to prepare the coach for a hasty escape. Brighton might be a good choice.

"Yes, I meet with him tomorrow morning at ten."

Caroline's mind whirred. As much as she desired it, a quick escape was most likely impossible. She was exhausted from the ball, and Darcy had just arrived. He would surely not want to go to Brighton, and Caroline would not care to leave him behind.

Persuasion was her only option.

"Must you rush, Charles?" she asked sweetly.

"It is only you that think it rushed. For me, it is perfect timing."

"But her mother! Her sisters! Terribly unsuitable; don't we all agree?"

Only Mrs. Hurst nodded her head. Mr. Hurst ignored the command, and Darcy sat removed, silently amused at Caroline's desperate and transparent performance.

She caught him staring at him and met his gaze. "Darcy, say something. Stop him."

"I cannot. Your brother has always been impulsive. Is there anything objectionable about the young woman's character?"

As it was Jane he was referring to, no flaws were readily proclaimed.

After a brief interlude of silence, Bingley said, "My apologies for deserting you tomorrow morning, my friend. You have free reign of the place in my absence."

"That is good of you, my man," Darcy smiled. "But please, point me to your library or book room and I will be a happy fellow. I have yet to discover it during my ramblings about the place."

Bingley's expression fell, knowing he was to disappoint his friend.

"There is no library. Or books."

Darcy raised a singular eyebrow.

"No books?"

"I am sorry. There were very few personal possessions included in the lease. I assumed you would have brought your own books?"

"As my travels have extended beyond my foresight, I have finished all the books that I packed. The library at Rosings was my savior."

"Mr. Darcy, do not fret about the lack of books. We can send someone to the mercantile tomorrow to get you a novel. Remember, we are your good friends, happy that you are here, and we will provide ample entertainment for you in Bingley's absence tomorrow, won't we? We have the archery set," Mrs. Hurst offered.

"I could use a good ride," Mr. Hurst offered. "We can go out in the morning."

"And we are anxious for news of Miss Georgiana," Caroline said. "Some time reserved to hear the news of her health and well-being would be cheering."

Bingley turned to Darcy. "So you see, Darcy! You have plenty of friends. Your day shall not be dull."

"I am sorry to require so much attention," Darcy said. "Although I am always content with a book, a day spent with friends is always much preferred."

***

Undeterred by his sisters' repeated attempts to persuade him otherwise, Bingley rode off to Longbourn the next morning. While he was away, Darcy, Caroline, and Mrs. Hurst convened for a walk around the grounds. It was a bright day, and the late fall air was warmer than usual—an inducement toward wandering, Darcy said.

Bingley's obsession with Miss Jane was uppermost on all of their minds.

"He has greatly surprised me twice in the past few months," said Mrs. Hurst. "First, Netherfield, now Miss Bennet. I only hope he is not suffering from some type of manic episode."

"Netherfield can be disposed of easily; Miss Bennet should be just as disposable," Caroline observed.

"I have not given up hope of Bingley and Georgiana being happy together," Darcy confessed.

Caroline took a quick look at Darcy. His expression was familiarly stoic.

"There is no engagement as of yet with Miss Jane, which is a relief. But given the hasty pace of Bingley's recent decisions, I cannot rest easily," Caroline said. "There is an entail on Longbourn, which makes their situation more desperate."

"Ahh, indeed. Tricky things, those entails," Darcy said.

"I cannot help but feel that we chose better for him than he did for himself, for Miss Bennet and Netherfield will always pale in comparison to Miss Darcy and Chipperton," pointed out Mrs. Hurst. "And Mrs. Bennet has an air of a mercenary about her."

"It is my experience that it is the rare instance when the eldest daughter is not trained in the same manner," Darcy observed.

Caroline was pleased to hear such wisdom flowing from Darcy and agreed with him by saying, "I had hoped another season or two of my brother and your sister being thrown together would do the trick. But this sizeable passion for Netherfield has upset our plans."

"Perhaps we should not assume the match with Miss Bennet is a foregone conclusion. As I am just as driven to ensure my sister's happiness as you are to ensure your brother's, perhaps we should all convene back at Pemberley. Georgiana returns soon from Rosings, and we shall want company during the festive season. It will require tearing Bingley away from here, which might please everyone."

"A timely separation from Miss Bennet may be beneficial," Caroline suggested, feigning silent consideration while inside she rejoiced at the idea of exchanging Christmas in Netherfield for one at Pemberley.

"But will he leave her?" Mrs. Hurst wondered. "Bingley seems to have grown up a bit over the past month or two; I fear he may not be as malleable as before."

"He may resist, but then he must be persuaded," Caroline

persisted. "I may seek your help in that regard, if it comes to that," she said to Darcy.

"I'll mention the idea to him directly in a day or two," Darcy promised.

"Now, Mr. Darcy. Entertain us with some news of Pemberley," Caroline urged.

Darcy, who could not resist speaking about his favorite subject, gladly obliged.

***

"Please, I'd like you to get to know her. She is all amiability and modesty despite her beauty," Bingley said to Darcy over a pint in the Meryton Ale House after Darcy had raised the issue of Miss Bennet.

"Your sisters have some concerns. Something about an entail?" Darcy related.

"Sorry business. Yes, it's true. But my sisters always have something to say."

"An entail is a tough situation for the survivors."

"True, but how can Miss Jane help this accident of birth? It does not make her unworthy. Notice that my sisters make no claim against Miss Bennet's character."

"On that, you are correct. Perhaps it is their controlling natures that you are up against?" Darcy wondered.

"You see it too?" Bingley asked. "I am used to their

complaints, but with Miss Jane, I cannot agree with their point of view."

"It will be your choice in the end; being a man requires choosing what is best for you and not what most pleases others," Darcy advised.

"Yes, I am beginning to understand that now more than ever," Bingley said, taking a swig from his mug and silently considering Darcy's statements for a moment. "Please, Darcy, accompany me when I next call on her and see for yourself. I would greatly value your opinion, gathered independently and not culled from my sisters' gossip."

"Very well," Darcy agreed. "Although my opinion will be my own, not influenced by your sisters or you," he warned.

"Fair enough," Bingley agreed, confident that there was no fault to be found with Miss Bennet and eager for Darcy to be his ally in that regard. Sensing that the timing was not right, Darcy put off extending his offer that they decamp to Pemberley for the holidays. He did not wish to anger his old friend by judging Miss Bennet prematurely or suggest he leave town when he most clearly wanted to stay near Jane.

The agreed-upon visit to the Bennets was set for the next day. Bingley and Darcy arrived to a somewhat empty Longbourn. Jane and Mary were at home, but Mrs. Bennet and Lydia and Kitty were at the shops, and Elizabeth out taking the air. Darcy observed the couple silently; the small group was easier for him to handle, and Jane and Mary were well-mannered hosts.

As happened in a country neighborhood, the conversation drifted to people that Darcy didn't know or care about. Not having much to contribute to the conversation, he observed Miss Bennet closely, and what he saw concerned him. He found her manner to be so even-keeled that he began to suspect it was a performance. She seemed to issue the same serene smile to everyone in the room.

Surely, were she in love with his friend, that smile would reach her eyes more deeply? Would she not occasionally blush to be in the presence of a deep love?

Yet none of these physical reactions were evident upon her person. Darcy did not want to think that she could be playing a game with Bingley, but now the possibility must be considered. After a good forty-five-minute visit, Darcy coughed into his handkerchief—the pre-arranged signal that he and Bingley had devised to indicate it was time to depart. Darcy had seen enough to convince him that Bingley's future happiness was in danger and that Miss Bennet's love might be more for Netherfield and its comforts than for its current master. Longbourn was a significant downgrade in scale from Netherfield. With four unattached sisters underfoot, Darcy understood the necessity of unloading the eldest on an eligible man such as Bingley.

He also knew that taking Bingley's sisters' side against Miss Jane would hurt his friend, but Darcy did not shy from uncomfortable truths. He would be gentle with Bingley. Perhaps taking Bingley away for a holiday visit to Pemberley was all that would be needed to dampen Miss Jane's mercenary affection for

Bingley.

The pair stood up and said their goodbyes.

After leaving the drawing room, they paused briefly in the entryway to put on their hats and button their overcoats when, suddenly, the front door flew open.

A shock of cold air accompanied Elizabeth Bennet as she burst into the entryway. She was required to stop abruptly in surprise at the unexpected presence of Bingley and Darcy in the crowded space.

"Goodness, I didn't know we had company," she exclaimed.

"Just leaving, Miss Elizabeth," Bingley explained. Turning to Darcy, he said, "You remember my friend from the ball, but I didn't introduce you properly. May I present Miss Jane's sister, Miss Elizabeth Bennet. Mr. Fitzwilliam Darcy."

Elizabeth nodded and said, "Good afternoon, Mr. Darcy, Mr. Bingley. I am sorry to have missed the call. I was out walking."

Darcy found himself wholly taken aback to encounter the lovely songbird from the Netherfield ball and, for a moment, words escaped him. How could he have been so unaware that this young woman was the sister of Miss Bennet? But, of course, he paid no attention to the names or the relations of any of the Meryton residents.

Suddenly, the tenor of the call changed dramatically for him, and he wished he wasn't standing there, dressed in his coat and his hat and gloves, on his way out to the waiting carriage. How he wanted to linger in that moment, but Bingley was halfway out the front door, and Darcy had no choice but to follow. He tipped his hat to Miss Elizabeth and then walked out stiffly to the carriage, his posture straight but his heart beating rapidly in an uncommon combination of surprise and delight and regret.

He immediately forgot the words of caution regarding Miss Jane that he had meant to issue during the drive home. Instead, he listened half-heartedly as Bingley effused about Jane, and scolded himself internally for being so quick to signal to end the visit. If he had only delayed for a quarter of an hour longer then surely the sister would have joined them in the drawing room.

What was her name again?

Elizabeth.

Elizabeth, he repeated to himself.

How lovely!

How he would like to see her again, and he began to think of ways they could be in the same place. Just as the carriage pulled up to Netherfield, he found himself blurting out, "We should probably call again on the Bennets when the rest of the family is home. Miss Elizabeth looked sorry to have not been included. It would not be right to allow her to believe that we took any pleasure in excluding her."

Bingley looked stricken. "Oh, dear. No, that was never my intention. Darcy, you are always the epitome of grace and manners. Yes, Miss Elizabeth has always been kind to me, and I do not mean to slight her or exclude her from our calls."

"We should call again this week. Don't let it go too long,"

Darcy advised. "Perhaps we should write to ensure they are all at home next time before we call. That is the best way to avoid offense to the parents as well."

"Agreed," Bingley said quickly. Then, before exiting the carriage, he looked at Darcy and said, "And Miss Jane? You liked her very much, didn't you? I can tell."

Darcy hastily decided that criticizing Miss Jane was not necessary at the moment. Her sister seemed absolutely intriguing, so perhaps Jane appealed to Bingley in the same way? Perhaps there were qualities in Miss Jane that revealed themselves over time?

"Yes, I did like her," Darcy found himself saying. "From what I could surmise from the brief call, she is a charming young woman. I would be able to say more after meeting her again." He thought that he would say anything in order to engineer another meeting with the songbird of Longbourn.

Bingley grinned from ear to ear.

As advised, Bingley wrote to the Bennets inquiring if the whole family would be home if they called the day after tomorrow. His inquiry was met with a rapid, encouraging reply penned by Mrs. Bennet.

"No, thank you," replied Caroline, and Mrs. Hurst echoed the same sentiment when asked if they would join the excursion to Longbourn.

"We have seen the place once; I dare say that will suffice until the next half-moon," Mrs. Hurst laughed. Darcy was relieved. He suddenly realized how ever-present Miss Bingley was with regard to his movements. In his gut, he knew Caroline would tease him were she to notice his curiosity about the second-eldest Bennet daughter.

With the exception of Mr. Bennet, who scheduled himself to be out, the entire Bennet family sat poised and eager when the two gentlemen next called. There was a heightened air of excitement due to the honor they felt to be in the presence of Mr. Darcy. Darcy, however, held back, conversing rarely. But when coffee was served, and the party rose from their seats to take their cups from the table, Darcy found a way to put himself near Elizabeth.

He said, "Miss Elizabeth, may I compliment you on your lovely performance the other evening? I was quite impressed."

For a moment, Elizabeth was surprised by his comment. She thought Bingley's friend to be darkly handsome, but she remembered only seeing him once or twice at the beginning of the ball, but not at all after a certain point. She did not remember seeing him in the crowd while she performed. His formal manners contrasted with Bingley's casual, yet always impeccable, manners, and she found the pairing between the affable Bingley and reserved Darcy interesting.

She murmured a quick, "Thank you. I am glad to hear my performance pleased you and equally as surprised."

"Tell me, who is your teacher?" Darcy inquired.

"I do not have a teacher, Mr. Darcy. I am self-taught and sing for my own enjoyment or as a favor to someone whom I cannot refuse."

Sensing the young lady was modest as well as gifted, he said only, "You have quite a pleasing tone to your voice."

He excused himself and walked to the table. Having said his piece, he stayed quiet for the rest of the visit, but in his looks and expression seemed engaged by the company. His observations of Miss Elizabeth continued throughout the call, and her behavior and cleverness in speaking impressed him greatly.

# *CHAPTER TEN*

Sir William Lucas and Mr. Darcy spoke only briefly at the Netherfield ball, as Darcy was spent from his day of traveling, but the encounter left Sir William wanting more. As Sir William considered himself the reigning elder statesmen of Meryton, it behooved him to host an evening in honor of the neighborhood's newest and most distinguished arrival. This invitation was encouraged, albeit possibly suggested, by Lady Lucas, who feared that Bingley was lost as a romantic option for her eldest daughter. However, an important man like Darcy might appreciate a sensible, level-headed young lady like Charlotte, who could run Pemberley with economy.

The dinner party was thrown on the following weekend and required much planning and expense, an investment the couple thought necessary, considering all the benefits a man like Darcy could give to their Charlotte. But the party had barely been underway for an hour when Lady Lucas first noticed Darcy staring at Miss Elizabeth. His gaze settled on her repeatedly while drinks were served before dinner. She noticed that Darcy approached Miss Elizabeth and fixed himself near her, and that he listened intently to everything she said. And, when the assembled party raised their glasses in a toast led by Sir William, she noticed that Darcy took a sidewise glance at

Elizabeth before he sipped.

Alarmed, Lady Lucas slipped into the dining room and hurriedly switched the place cards, as Miss Elizabeth was originally slated to sit across the table from Darcy.  Instead, she strategically seated Elizabeth on the same side of the table as Darcy, far to his left with several guests spaced in-between, virtually out of sight, and the non-threatening Mr. Bennet was seated across from Darcy.

As any mother would, she seated Mr. Darcy and Charlotte together for dinner. She caught glimpses of Charlotte and Darcy speaking comfortably and naturally to each other throughout the courses and congratulated herself on the quick switch. As Darcy drank and ate, he seemed completely at ease, and Lady Lucas found herself sighing with relief.

But after dinner, Darcy paid no further attention to Charlotte. Instead, she saw Darcy pull Sir William aside and have a short conversation, all the while staring at Elizabeth.

Immediately upon quitting Darcy, Sir William approached Elizabeth.

"Do indulge us all with one of your beautiful performances at the pianoforte," he said to her.

Elizabeth looked across the room. Darcy was watching her and Sir William converse. She was very conscious that Darcy seemed to have initiated this request, and she demurred, feeling slightly embarrassed by the attention.

"Thank you very much, that is very kind of you, but I couldn't bore the party with my songs," she explained.

"It is not a bore. And Mr. Darcy desires a song."

Still Elizabeth hesitated. "Your Charlotte has a lovely voice. I would be happy to duet with her. We have practiced together many times."

"He asked for you, specifically." Sir William's eyes were twinkling. "I hate to disappoint my guests."

Mrs. Bennet, who had observed the encounter, approached the duo.

"Sir William, is there something that I can help you with?"

"Only help me persuade your Miss Elizabeth to sing. A special request from one of our guests; I hate to disappoint him." Sir William looked over to where he had left Darcy.

"Why, of course, my Elizabeth will sing for you," Mrs. Bennet said. Placing her hand upon Elizabeth's forearm in a tight grip, she hissed softly, "Now, Lizzy, be a dear and sing or no pin money for a month."

Smiling, Elizabeth elbowed her way out of her mother's grasp and turned to Sir William. "Thank you, Sir William, for the invitation to play. I am ready when you are."

"Splendid. Let me draw my guests' attention," he replied, and, like a maestro, he clapped his hands and motioned his arms so that the ensuing conversations all stalled, and the room fell quiet.

In the stillness, Sir William simply made a motion toward the pianoforte, where Elizabeth was now seated tensely on the bench, aware that all eyes were upon her but conscious of only one man's gaze. She could sense his power—how at his command virtual strangers hurried to fulfill his requests. Feeling outmaneuvered, she bowed her head, placed her fingers on the desired keys and began.

Polite applause followed her performance, and Sir William then pushed forward Charlotte to duet with Elizabeth. Elizabeth gladly made room for her friend on the bench, and they expertly performed two favorites they sang together often. Their performance was joyful and exuberant, and there were shouts for more when they finished. However, as soon as the notes of the song faded, Mary Bennet crowded the pianoforte, anxious to replace Elizabeth and Charlotte as the entertainment and gain her share of attention. Elizabeth greatly desired to be away from the staring gaze of Mr. Darcy, and she rose from the bench and slipped around the piano.

But she could not avoid him. He stepped directly into her path and said, "Miss Elizabeth, that was delightful".

"Thank you, Mr. Darcy. But you are well-traveled and have a home in London. Certainly, you have heard better."

"I have heard many a performance in London concert halls," he said. "That makes me qualified to comment on your playing. You must have had a marvelous instructor."

"As I said the other day, I do not have a teacher, sir. I only sing for my own enjoyment."

"Then you have an ear for music. A wonderful gift!"

"Yes," she agreed, slightly conscious of the furtive glances of her friends and neighbors. How they would stare and embarrass her! Thankfully, Mary began pounding a dirge-like tune, and the need to give her their full attention halted her discourse with Darcy. She was aware, however, that the man did not make any attempt to move away from her, and she was therefore obliged to remain standing mutely beside him for the duration of Mary's performance.

But no sooner had the music ended than Darcy turned to Elizabeth, nodded, and said swiftly, "Thank you for your time. I must say my goodbyes."

"Thank you," Elizabeth found herself responding in kind, but he did not stay to hear her response.

"I should be glad if I were you for Darcy taking leave," Charlotte said to Elizabeth as she linked arms with her friend and started to walk with her. "Now you may enjoy the rest of the evening without the entire party watching you. I know how his attention must have bothered you, as you are the one young lady I know who will remain sensible around a man of wealth and not let a simple request to play music turn your head."

"You know me well, dear friend. Were it not for the very strong threat from my mother, and my desire to please your father, I would have fought harder to sit it out."

The two women entered the next room, where they immediately found themselves face to face with Caroline Bingley. She had a curious look about her, the meaning of which Elizabeth could only interpret as simple dislike.

"Very well done, Miss Elizabeth," Caroline said with disinterest.

Elizabeth smiled and thanked her.

"I am sure you are as curious as the rest of us as to what Mr.

Darcy must mean by paying you so much attention. My sister and I were just discussing how oddly he is behaving toward you."

"Oh?" Elizabeth responded. "Is he?"

"But of course. He is the finest gentleman of our acquaintance. We are good friends, having stayed with him and his sister this summer at Pemberley. His holdings are quite grand, I can assure you, and the man's reputation is irreproachable. His generosity with his household staff and tenants is lauded throughout the county. That is why we are so utterly confused as to what he must be thinking by singling you out as the object of his attention throughout the evening."

"I hardly know Mr. Darcy's mind."

'But what did he say to you?" she asked impertinently.

Elizabeth paused a moment to reflect on her short conversation with Darcy, wondering why Miss Bingley seemed to feel *she* was owed an explanation. "He seems to think I have a musical gift," Elizabeth informed her. "Although I do not understand why. My singing seems quite ordinary, or so I've been told."

"Does he?" Caroline said with a laugh. "I will ask him on the way home what it is about your voice that he finds so fascinating."

"Excuse me, so sorry to interrupt," Sir William said as he suddenly appeared at their side. "Miss Bingley, your party is asking for you. Mr. Hurst is unwell, and Mr. Darcy is anxious that you all be on your way home."

"Unwell? Oh dear," Caroline sighed. "Thank you, Sir William, for the lovely evening and your hospitality."

"This way, my lady," he said, offering his arm. "I'll get you through the crowd." Caroline latched onto Sir William's arm and left with no parting acknowledgment.

Charlotte and Elizabeth stood silently for a few moments until Charlotte smiled mischievously at Elizabeth. "My goodness!" Charlotte laughed softly. "She seemed quite eager to tell us how very unspecial we all are."

Charlotte turned around to take a quick glance over her shoulder, then she drew Elizabeth close and whispered, "I have it on authority that Miss Bingley has set her cap for Mr. Darcy, but that Mr. Darcy is completely uninterested."

Elizabeth grinned from ear to ear. "Who is your source?"

"Her brother-in-law, Mr. Hurst, said as much to my father at the ball."

"So she is not protecting Darcy, merely saving him for herself."

"Yes, and it appears that Mr. Darcy's attentions to you have rankled Miss Bingley."

"Indeed. She seems positively possessive of the man," Elizabeth concurred.

"She must be frightfully on edge every time Mr. Darcy breathes in a young lady's direction," Charlotte says.

"Yes. I do not trust her."

"Neither do I," Charlotte murmured. "She is so unlike her brother."

"What a strange mix families are," Elizabeth wondered aloud.

"How the same setting can produce such significantly different personalities. I see it amongst my own sisters as well."

***

Yet, despite Charlotte's tales, Caroline Bingley was not overly anxious about Darcy's attentions to Elizabeth. During the following days, when they were contained to their own society at Netherfield, it was easy for Caroline to reassure herself that the lowly Bennet girls could offer nothing to a man like Darcy.

Life at Netherfield had its own quiet rhythm, and the days they spent without interference from the outside world always seemed to pass with such pleasure. At least that was Caroline's view. Mr. Darcy was always quickly lost in a book, yet after dinner he would always take the time to discuss what he enjoyed about the novel with all of them, sometimes leaving the finished copy for Miss Bingley to read.

They often reminisced about their summer at Pemberley, and he would read aloud from Georgiana's letters depicting her life at Rosings. But, four days after the dinner at Sir William's, Darcy hurriedly entered the Netherfield drawing room.

"News from my cousin Col. Fitzwilliam," Darcy began. "Their visit at Rosings has come to an abrupt end, as my aunt has fallen ill and so, apparently, has my cousin Anne."

"Goodness, how alarming," Mrs. Hurst exclaimed. "Not the influenza?"

"It is something worse for my aunt. A sore throat so painful she cannot speak. She has been reduced to writing down all her commands. My cousin has very rightly decided that it would be best for him and Georgiana to depart lest risk coming down with the same illness. Apparently, my aunt has agreed to the wisdom of a quick departure."

"He must leave; he must protect Miss Darcy," Bingley exclaimed, suddenly very alarmed.

"Yes, they may already be on the road. There is good news in his missive, however, as they are heading here to see me. They should be here late tomorrow," said Darcy.

"Miss Darcy here?" Miss Bingley exclaimed. "How wonderful!"

Bingley glanced around the room with pride.

"While I am sorry to hear that your aunt and cousin are unwell, there is no company like familiar faces. Oh, I do hope Miss Darcy is pleased with Netherfield when she arrives. Caroline, we must prepare rooms for them. I don't know what to do to make it nice but spare no expense."

"Please, no special preparations are necessary for Georgiana," Darcy said.

"No, I insist," Bingley stood with an air of determination. "This is what I've always wanted, to have a home to share with my best friends. I am beyond delighted at the news."

The imminent arrival of Georgiana and Col. Fitzwilliam sent Bingley into a flurry of anxious activity. He instructed the cook that their meals should not be limited by budgetary concerns. He inspected the two guest bedrooms himself on their worthiness for such honored guests. He urged his sisters to fill Netherfield with flowers from the hothouse, and he ordered the maids to polish the windows and floors until they sparkled.

Caroline and Darcy observed his ministrations with hopefulness, for neither had given up on the idea of Bingley and Georgiana marrying.

With Netherfield in order and his guests due to arrive, Bingley paced anxiously before the drawing room windows as darkness fell.

"They should be here soon," he said, glancing at the mantel clock.

Darcy laid down his book calmly. "My cousin is rarely off when estimating his arrival."

"Yes, yes. Good man, he is," Bingley nodded eagerly, walking in circles around the room with his hands clasped behind his back. He stopped to straighten the china figurine of a shepherdess and then picked up an odd scrap from the carpet.

Caroline sat placidly with her hands folded in front of her.

"I have had a thought," she announced.

All eyes turned toward her.

"For their own health, it may be unwise to accept callers over the next few days. Although I know how you admire Meryton society," she said, smiling at her brother as she spoke, "it would be wise to make sure that both Miss Darcy and Col. Fitzwilliam are not about to come down with the same illness."

Darcy nodded. "The fatigue of the trip and the recent exposure to the ill air of Rosings may have weakened their constitutions," he added. "Bingley, your sister makes great sense."

"Then we shall be confined to our own company," Bingley agreed. "Miss Darcy's continued good health is my most fervent wish. We shall not tire her; instead, she will rest and not be disturbed by company until we are assured she is in perfect health."

Mrs. Hurst glanced across the room at her sister, and their eyes met in silent acknowledgement of Caroline's plotting.

"I, for one, will appreciate the break from socializing," Mrs. Hurst said. "How easy the company was at Pemberley over the summer."

"Pemberley was bliss," Caroline agreed, glancing over at Darcy for him to assert a similar sentiment, but Darcy was distracted by the flicker of a coach light visible between the trees on the front park of Netherfield.

"Ah," he said, rising and reaching for his pocket watch to confirm the time. "It appears they are here and five minutes early."

With joy, the party rose and filed out into the entry hall. Bingley threw open the doors of Netherfield and skipped quickly down the steps, oblivious to the chill evening air as the coach carrying Georgiana traveled the last few lengths of the drive and stopped before them.

# *CHAPTER ELEVEN*

After a spirited reunion and a full meal with courses of fish and pheasant, potatoes and peas, followed by a favorite pudding, the contented party moved into the drawing room. There, Col. Fitzwilliam and Georgiana detailed the goings-on at Rosings. "She has painted the drawing room a very bright yellow," Georgiana told them. "It was quite a transformation."

"How stylish," Caroline said. "I confess I do not keep up with the latest in interiors, having no home of my own to implement new ideas."

"Perhaps someday not too long into the future that may change?" Col. Fitzwilliam wondered aloud, smiling at Caroline.

Caroline returned the smile and then stole a glance at Darcy. When she was the mistress of Pemberley, she planned to increment change slowly so as not to disrespect the memory of Lady Anne. But several rooms needed an overhaul, of that she was certain.

"Pemberley does not follow fashion," Darcy said.

"Only because Mamma has been gone for so long—that is why nothing has been changed or updated," Georgiana protested. "I would like to see a yellow room at Pemberley. My new sitting room, perhaps? You would indulge me one room, wouldn't you, my sweet brother?"

"Pemberley change? But it is perfect the way it is!" Bingley exclaimed.

Darcy chuckled softly. "We can talk about paint colors. But painting and such updates are a project for the spring, don't you agree?"

Col. Fitzwilliam offered, "I imagine we might get used to a few changes in Pemberley, a little at a time so as not to rock our sensibilities."

"Why fuss with inherited grandeur?" Mrs. Hurst asked. "Don't average folks buy tickets to tour it for that very reason?"

"This is a pretty room," Georgiana commented, glancing about. "You must get plenty of sunlight from those tall windows during the day."

"Yes, yes!" Bingley responded. "It was what sold me on the place. I tell you, I took one tour about the rooms and grounds and was absolutely spellbound by its charm. Of course, it is no Pemberley, but the scale is perfect for my needs at this time. And the neighbors are some of the best around. You will see."

"Yes, Bingley, it suits you. It's no Chipperton," Georgiana agreed.

"Let me temper my brother's enthusiasm for the neighbors so as not to raise your expectations," said Caroline. "They are perfectly ordinary country folk, the likes of which I am sure Miss Georgiana has met in her travels."

Darcy cleared his throat. "There will be plenty of time to

meet the locals after you two have recovered from your journey. Until then, we have nothing but quiet days planned."

"Here, here, I like the sound of that," Col. Fitzwilliam said. "Aunt Catherine likes a constant flow of activity. It makes her anxious when things are too quiet. I am ready for a respite."

"Darcy is right. You must rest after the journey and keep to your room as long as it pleases you to do so. We can take the air around Netherfield, but the plan is to stay to ourselves for the next few days," Bingley looked admiringly at Georgiana, and Darcy was pleased to see his attentiveness aimed toward her.

"That sounds heavenly, as it has been hectic lately," Georgiana said and, stifling a yawn, added, "It is late. Perhaps we should call it a night?" Caroline and Mrs. Hurst agreed.

"Let us walk you upstairs," offered Caroline.

"Thank you kindly, for I am not certain I can find my room again on my own," Georgiana agreed.

Darcy said, "We'll burn the candle a little longer together. Have a good night, ladies."

The next day, Miss Darcy did as advised and rested happily in her chamber. Caroline and Mrs. Hurst checked in on her. They fluffed the pillows, adjusted the drapes, stoked the fire, and insisted that Georgiana send word the minute she desired company. Assured by Georgiana that she was perfectly content, Caroline and Mrs. Hurst then joined the men, as Bingley had promised Col. Fitzwilliam a tour of the grounds.

There had been a frost overnight, and the cooler temperature spurred them to walk swiftly, but the sun was bright and clear, and Netherfield's trees showed off their best winter silhouettes. After completing a brisk circuit around the grounds, the group hurriedly retreated to the warmth of the drawing room. Presently, Bingley excused himself to deal with pressing household matters and Darcy took leave to check on Georgiana.

"Please let her know we will be happy to be up whenever she wishes," Caroline reminded Darcy. That left Col. Fitzwilliam to the care of Caroline and the Hursts.

"Tell me a little more about your impressions of Hertfordshire of which you alluded to last night," Col. Fitzwilliam said to Miss Bingley, by way of making polite conversation. "Your brother seems over the moon about the place but was I correct in sensing that your enthusiasm is less than his?"

"You have a keen sense of understanding," Caroline complimented him. "Allow me the liberty to be frank, Col. Fitzwilliam, as I trust you are as discrete as your cousin."

"As, indeed," he nodded solemnly.

"My brother lacks discernment when mingling in unfamiliar society," she explained. "More than once, I have had to make the decision to remove him from our situation due to the unsuitable women to which he attached himself. I am sorry to say that I fear we have encountered the same situation here at Netherfield."

"I am sorry to hear that. I sensed some displeasure in the society in your remarks last night, to be equally as frank."

"He fancies himself in love again here too," said Caroline.

"Who is the woman?"

"Miss Jane Bennet. Clearly the most beautiful young lady in town," Mrs. Hurst said.

"The only beautiful young lady," Caroline clarified. Mrs. Hurst laughed outright, and Caroline joined in.

"Yes, the only beautiful young lady in the area, to be precise," Mrs. Hurst corrected herself.

"What is wrong with this beautiful young lady then?" Col. Fitzwilliam asked.

Caroline sighed. "The same thing that is always wrong with them. Obviously looking for a rich man, only in this case, the situation is even more alarming. The family consists of five unmarried daughters, all out, and the home is entailed. So desperation drips off of the lot."

"Especially the mother," Mrs. Hurst added. "So indiscrete."

Col. Fitzwilliam nodded in agreement. "Ah, I see."

"It was our dream that Bingley and Miss Darcy form an attachment. This folly on Bingley's part of coming to Hertfordshire is still hard for me to comprehend," Caroline said. "It does nothing but distract from our plans for him."

"I know you had hopes he would lease in Derbyshire," Col. Fitzwilliam said.

"Yes, as did Darcy." Caroline shook her head.

"Although, this is a charming estate," Col. Fitzwilliam said. "I can see its allure."

"Sometimes, I quite like it here," Mrs. Hurst concurred.

Caroline gave her sister a sharp look and said, "Sister, don't tease me so. I have a persistent bad feeling about this place, as if everything is spinning out of control."

"Not what you would have picked for yourself?" Col. Fitzwilliam guessed.

"No," Caroline agreed quietly. "But it is much more tolerable when the Darcy family is here," she added.

"Is it?" Col. Fitzwilliam laughed happily in response. "I am glad to hear it." He smiled broadly across the room at Caroline.

"I think Bingley said the cook is baking the famous iced buns from Pemberley for tea today, to entice Miss Darcy," said Caroline. "Perhaps love will bloom amongst them in the next few days. I remain hopeful."

"Speaking of food, I do wish they would call luncheon. I am famished," said Mrs. Hurst.

"Let me go check on that for you," Col. Fitzwilliam offered, standing up.

"Oh, you are too kind," Mrs. Hurst said.

"Nonsense, it is no trouble," he smiled.

As soon as he was gone, Mrs. Hurst raised her eyebrows and blinked her sister's way.

"Now there is a man as fine as Darcy. Better in some ways, I might guess, for he falls easily into conversation and is not as reserved."

"Do you think so?" Caroline replied. "I hadn't noticed. I think only of my future at Pemberley."

"You should consider him, even though he is a second son. You are rich enough for both of you."

"Such comments depress my spirits."

"Why? It is not my intention."

"Because I cannot take my eye off of the target where Darcy is concerned."

"But it is going nowhere!" Mrs. Hurst said with exasperation.

"I don't know that," Caroline rebuffed her.

"If I were you," she said. "I would hedge my bets. It's a fine family, and if you cannot win Darcy, Col. Fitzwilliam will keep you Darcy adjacent. Either way, you will not lose access to Pemberley."

Caroline reddened and turned away. Her sister would be maddeningly honest at times. But her sister had also settled for a local man with less than half the wealth and none of Darcy's impressive dignity. No, Caroline said to herself. She would not entertain thoughts of winning mere proximity to Pemberley. She must have it all.

***

"How delicious! And just like Mrs. Reynolds bakes," Georgiana exclaimed after one bite of the iced buns that Bingley had so proudly presented to her when she joined them in the drawing room for tea.

"Do you like them?" he inquired anxiously.

"Very much, so," she nodded.

"They are remarkably similar," Col. Fitzwilliam agreed. "Mrs. Reynolds isn't hiding out in the kitchen and going to appear and surprise us all, is she?" he asked, making a ploy of looking toward the door in anticipation.

"No, she isn't here. But I did make a point of having her dictate the ingredients and measurements to Caroline before we left Pemberley," Bingley said proudly.

"Bravo," said Col. Fitzwilliam.

"Now, Darcy, you promised to read aloud to us all after tea. We are so anxious to hear what happens next," Georgiana said.

"I did, didn't I? I will if it pleases everyone else," Darcy said, looking around the room to gain approval.

"Absolutely," said Mr. Hurst, reclining back in his chair in contentment. Five minutes hence, he had nodded off to sleep.

After reading aloud for the better part of an hour, Darcy put down the book. "That is all for now. So tell me, how are the two travelers feeling after this somewhat quiet day? Rested? Well-fed?"

Both Georgiana and Col Fitzwilliam declared themselves completely recovered from the rush of their departure and journey.

"Perhaps in a day or two, we can go to the shops? I'd like to see more of this little town that Bingley fell in love with," Georgiana asked, looking hopefully over to the two sisters.

"Yes, in a day or two. No rush, though," Darcy insisted. "These sore throats can come upon one quickly at this time of year, and to my estimation, it feels like rain coming; does anyone else agree?" Bingley nodded in agreement, and Mrs. Hurst complained that her knuckles ached, a clear predictor of precipitation.

"Miss Darcy, as for the shops, let me assure you that you are missing nothing. They lack the charm of those in Lambton," Caroline said.

"Oh, dear, I am sorry to hear that they do not please you," Georgiana replied.

"I would love to hear some music. Can you play for us?" Darcy asked his sister.

"Please do," urged Mrs. Hurst. "Play that tune you used to play at Pemberley. You know the one, dah dah dah, dah dah dah," she hummed.

Georgiana furrowed her brow. "I think I know what you mean," she laughed, and she made her way over to the pianoforte and commenced playing.

"No, no, not exactly what I remembered," Mrs. Hurst objected, stopping Georgiana.

"How about this one instead?" Georgiana offered, and several bars in, Mrs. Hurst was clapping her plump hands excitedly, her expectations met.

Caroline chuckled at the scene. She glanced around the room at her companions and studied each one briefly as she listened. Darcy looked more content than she had seen him in a long time as he gazed at his sister with deep affection. Col. Fitzwilliam looked almost handsome in the dying light of the afternoon, Mrs. Hurst wore a delighted smile as she hummed along with the melody, and Bingley was gazing at Miss Darcy with a look of adoration that quite warmed

Caroline's heart and raised her hopes. This was the company she most preferred to keep, and she wished desperately that these days together could go on forever, without any intrusion from social-climbing outsiders to shatter their perfect simplicity.

# *CHAPTER TWELVE*

However, despite Caroline's wishes, the pleasant mood did not carry over to the morrow. As Darcy predicted, the next day delivered grey skies, steady rain, and soggy grounds. Boredom reared its ugly head by mid-morning, as no walks could be taken. No one was in the mood to read aloud or play music. They settled for cards and played half-heartedly, feigning enthusiasm.

"I feel a general ennui today," complained Georgiana, standing at the window and sighing.

"You are not unwell, are you?" Darcy quickly inquired; concern etched across his face.

"No, no," she insisted. "Only bored."

"I suspect today's rain makes staying indoors feel like a punishment, as opposed to yesterday when you stayed in because you wanted to," opined Col Fitzwilliam.

"If I had not stayed in so much yesterday, I would welcome a rainy day," Georgiana said, pressing her forehead against the windowpane. After standing still for a few moments, she then turned to glance at the mantel clock. "Only a quarter to eleven? What a long day it is already."

"Come and play another hand with us," Darcy urged. "I am sure your luck will change."

"No, thank you," she said and turned back to stare out the window at the rain.

Darcy and Col. Fitzwilliam exchanged looks.

"Tell us more about your time at Rosings," Mrs. Hurst said in an effort to engage her. "Any more funny tales of that new clergyman?"

"Oh, yes, Mr. Collins," Col. Fitzwilliam said. "Quite the character."

"I am all out of stories, even stories about Mr. Collins. I've said everything to say about my time at Rosings," Georgiana replied, turning from the window with a prolonged sigh. She walked to the side table and flipped through a stack of fashion magazines on display.

"Those are mine. You are welcome to them," Caroline said sweetly.

"Thank you," Georgiana smiled, and she carried the stack to the settee, sat down, and began to flip through them.

A few minutes later, she stood up and returned the pile back to the table.

Darcy looked up from shuffling the cards. "Not to your liking?"

"I read them all last month at Rosings," she replied.

"Ah," he said, putting his attention back to the cards.

Georgiana returned to the settee, sat down and quietly

studied her fingernails. Darcy bit his lip as he dealt, then sat quietly as he studied his cards. He played a distracted hand, losing quickly, before getting up and excusing himself. He was gone from the room for more than a quarter of an hour, but when he returned, his spirits were much elevated, and he whistled to himself as he rejoined the table. Georgiana looked across the room at her brother, and he smiled broadly back at her. She returned a weak smile and went back to her brooding contemplation, this time putting her chin on her hand and closing her eyes.

Luncheon provided a necessary distraction, and the party lingered at the table longer than usual. Darcy consulted his pocket watch more than once, prompting Bingley to inquire if he had plans for the day.

"I do, as a matter of fact," Darcy stated simply.

Eyebrows were raised around the table.

"Care to share?" Hurst asked boldly.

Darcy chuckled but refused to indulge his tablemates. "Patience, my dear friend."

"I have no time for these little games," Caroline announced. "I am going upstairs to my room to digest."

"Splendid idea," said Mrs. Hurst, suddenly overcome by a sudden yawn as she rose to join her sister.

"I'll do the same," Georgiana shrugged, putting her napkin down on the table.

"We'll have iced buns again for tea," Bingley promised cheerfully.

"Oh good," Georgiana replied without enthusiasm as she pushed in her chair and followed the ladies upstairs.

With the ladies dispersed, the men sat silently at the table for the next hour, reading the papers and the post and sipping brandy. After a while, Darcy, upon glancing out the window, rose suddenly.

"Excuse me, friends, but my plan for the afternoon is about to come to fruition." He ran his hand through his thick hair and fiddled with his cuffs. Col. Fitzwilliam looked out the window and back at Darcy, having seen nothing out of the ordinary and possessing not a single guess as to what was behind the mischievous grin that suddenly possessed his cousin.

***

Georgiana was sitting at the window seat in her room, staring at the rivulets of rain coursing down the windowpane when a knock sounded on her door.

"Come in," she said softly.

"Miss Darcy, you are wanted by Mr. Darcy in the drawing room," said Miss Hanna.

"Thank you. I'll be down directly."

"Thank you, ma'am." Miss Hanna nodded and closed the door.

Georgiana rose from her perch, checked her appearance in the mirror, ran a brush through her hair, and walked out into the hall. She could see Miss Hanna at the far end of the opposite corridor, knocking on the doors of the Bingley sisters' rooms. As Georgiana descended the stairs, the sound of the pianoforte wafted up to meet her, and then someone began to sing. It was a female voice, pure and clear.

Curious and intrigued, Georgiana walked gingerly to the door of the drawing room and nudged it open. Inside were two young ladies whom she did not recognize, sitting together at the pianoforte. One was playing and singing while the other turned the pages. Bingley and Hurst occupied the two sets of chairs nearest the gentle fire, while Col. Fitzwilliam was seated on the settee with his back to her and his attention on the performance. Darcy stood against the mantel, transfixed by the performers, with a strange expression on his face. An expression Georgiana knew she'd never seen on her brother before.

An expression she had long wished to see on him whilst looking at a young lady.

Her movement into the room disturbed Darcy's trance, and she smiled broadly back at him. She took her place next to Col. Fitzwilliam on the settee and listened raptly until the end of the song. Immediately upon finishing, the two young ladies delved directly into a lively duet. Georgiana smiled and relaxed. Suddenly, the rainy day came alive.

Up in her room, Caroline Bingley was surprised and delighted to be summoned by Darcy. He must have an important topic to address, she decided, and she tried to anticipate his thinking. Perhaps he wanted to speak to her about moving on to Pemberley, as he had mentioned before? Surely, Miss Darcy's depressed mood today would make him question the suitability of keeping her there in such decidedly less grand surroundings than Pemberley.

Why, that must be it!

Mr. Darcy was a man that took action and delighted in pleasing his sister. So different than how Bingley treated her, Caroline thought. She imagined that, in a few days, she would be looking at herself in the mirror in one of Pemberley's comfortable guest rooms, preparing herself for a pleasant afternoon out of shopping and laughing in Lambton.

She took a few extra minutes to prepare before going down, splashing water on her face and dabbing scent at her wrists. She smoothed out her hair and made a few fetching faces at herself in the mirror, turning to admire how nicely the cut of her dress showed off her figure.

Satisfied, she entered the corridor and made her way toward the stairs. She heard the pianoforte immediately and then the vocals.

Why it must be Miss Darcy, cheered by the news of their imminent departure and now game to perform for all of them. How splendid!

As she drew nearer, she realized that she had heard the song before and recently.

But where?

Then it came to her—it was at Sir William's house party and sung by Miss Lucas and Miss Elizabeth Bennet.

She stopped to listen, straining her ear to hear. With every bar, her suspicions were confirmed, and a fury ignited within her.

How dare they!

Who did they think they were and how pushy was it of them to call uninvited, disturbing their peace and threatening Georgiana's health! Darcy must be livid, for it was he who had insisted that they keep to their own company this week for the sake of Miss Darcy's health.

She approached the drawing room full of indignation and prepared to back up Darcy in the uncomfortable task of asking them to leave. But when she opened the door, she was met with an astonishing scene. Before her was a rapt audience, dreamy expressions plastered on each and every face, with their gaze firmly centered on the two interlopers. She slipped into the room quietly so as not to disturb and looked around the room quickly, certain to find Mrs. Bennet sitting in one of the chairs. Thankfully, she was not present.

"How odd," Caroline mumbled to Georgiana as she squeezed onto the settee between her and Col. Fitzwilliam. He gallantly moved closer to the arm so as to not crowd Miss Bingley.

"Who let them in?" she said under her breath to Col. Fitzwilliam.

Col. Fitzwilliam chuckled softly and replied in a low tone, "They are the guests of Mr. Darcy." He watched with amusement as Caroline's expression hardened.

"I don't believe it," she said stiffly. Yet one glance at Darcy told her everything. He was leaning against the wall gazing admiringly at Miss Bennet as if they were the only two in the room. Caroline swallowed hard, a pit suddenly forming in her stomach. She sat, silently fuming until the song ended.

"Bravo!" said Darcy in a strong voice, leading the group in a round of applause.

Bingley stood up as he clapped and walked over to the young ladies.

"Thank you, thank you. My, that was excellent! Please, let me introduce you to my guest whom you have not yet had the pleasure of meeting." Charlotte and Elizabeth stood up and walked around the pianoforte to stand next to Bingley, who gestured to Georgiana.

"May I present Miss Georgiana Darcy. Here is Miss Charlotte Lucas and Miss Elizabeth Bennet, who were more than gracious to ride out in the rain today in order to provide us with an afternoon's entertainment and company," Bingley said with great enthusiasm.

Georgiana very willingly exchanged cordialities with the two young women, complimenting them on their performance.

"And you know Miss Bingley and Mrs. Hurst," Bingley continued, motioning toward Caroline and to Mrs. Hurst, who had just joined the group from upstairs.

"Good afternoon, Miss Lucas, Miss Elizabeth," Caroline said primly. "It was very good of you to come out in such weather. I can't imagine doing the same myself on such a day. You must have been extremely bored with whatever you were tasked with doing."

"Oh, no, on the contrary! We rode in such comfort in Mr. Darcy's carriage that we never noticed the rain," Miss Lucas said.

Turning to Mr. Darcy, she said, "Thank you again, Mr. Darcy. My father was more than willing to lend us his carriage."

Darcy nodded and walked toward the two women. "It is you I must thank for indulging us this afternoon without much notice. I am so appreciative that you were not otherwise engaged. My sister loves music, and we were all in need of a diversion. Miss Bennet, may I request an encore performance of the piece you played at the ball a few weeks ago?"

Elizabeth agreed readily and headed back to the pianoforte.

"Miss Lucas, please, sit here," Col. Fitzwilliam said, offering his seat next to Caroline. Charlotte gladly accepted, and Col. Fitzwilliam took a position behind them, in full view of all the room's occupants. Darcy wandered back to his previous position against the mantel as Elizabeth began her song, singing with confidence and clarity and entrancing the room.

When the last note ended, Darcy applauded the longest.

"Miss Elizabeth, that was wonderful. But please, come away from the instrument, for I do not mean for you to strain your voice. Bingley, is it about time for tea? We must not let Miss Elizabeth become parched or feel that we have overworked her," Darcy said.

Caroline endeavored greatly not to roll her eyes at Darcy's comment, which she thought slightly ridiculous. Miss Elizabeth Bennet seemed as strong as a horse; surely her throat was in no danger after a few simple songs?

But Bingley adopted Darcy's worried tone as well and assured Darcy and Miss Elizabeth that tea was imminent. When it had not come in the next five minutes, he excused himself to expedite the staff but returned not a moment later, having met Miss Hanna and Miss Lilly in the hallway on their way with the refreshments. The bustle of laying the cloth on the table and carrying the trays of cups and the steaming pots of tea and arranging the plates of food consumed the room with activity.

Caroline watched Miss Lilly with resignation, as the presentation was decidedly not as elegant as she liked for guests.

"I am so sorry, but she cannot set the linen on straight," Caroline said to Georgiana after they had left. Indeed, the cloth puddled on the floor on one end of the table, noticeably uneven with the other side. "Details, details, details," Caroline whispered to herself.

Despite Caroline's fussing, the offerings were pleasing to all assembled. Mrs. Reynolds' iced buns, buttered toast, and ginger cake were passed around and eaten with much relish. Georgiana pleased Bingley greatly by again complimenting the iced buns and eating one and a half before declaring herself too full to continue. Charlotte and Elizabeth promised to sing one more song after the tea, spurring Darcy to insist that they were under no obligation to perform and must consider themselves welcome guests. Both women insisted they felt perfectly welcomed but had a new song to debut and were happy to deliver one more performance.

Presently, the time arrived when Miss Lucas and Miss Elizabeth were required to take their leave. Both promised to call again on Miss Darcy and to introduce her to their friends and families as soon as she was available. Darcy insisted on making a show of himself by escorting the ladies all the way to the door of their carriage when there was a perfectly capable footman to do the job instead, Caroline thought with disdain.

"The rain has stopped finally," Darcy declared, returning to the room after seeing off his guests.

"What a wonderful afternoon," Georgiana exclaimed happily. "Thank you! It was such a pleasant surprise."

"I thought you needed cheering up," he replied.

"Maybe we all did?" Georgiana said, looking around at her companions for agreement.

"Yes," Caroline said half-heartedly. "It was a wonderful afternoon. But I have a letter to write that has been neglected due to these musical distractions. Please excuse me."

Caroline endeavored to keep her composure as she took leave of the drawing room, but once inside the privacy of her chamber she gave in to her anger. What did Darcy mean by inviting Elizabeth Bennet into her home? What was his strange fascination with her, and why did he violate the pact they had made to ensure Miss Darcy's health with nothing but quiet days?

He had betrayed her trust by saying one thing and doing another, and worse, he seemed to relish doing it.

But there was a greater betrayal nagging at her. She thought of the way Darcy looked at Elizabeth, and she burned inside with jealousy. Darcy never looked at her like that.

Never.

And oh, how she longed for him to do so.

She had come to terms with his lack of passion for her, but she would not bear the blatant humiliation she felt that afternoon as she sat silently and watched as Darcy fawned over that creature. What could he mean by encouraging her? It was incomprehensible.

She sat on the edge of her bed, twisting the coverlet in her hands while her mind raced. She was so lost in thought that she did not notice the time passing, the sun going down, and not until Mrs. Hurst knocked on her door did she rouse herself from her dark thoughts.

"Are you ready to come down?" Mrs. Hurst asked through the door.

"I'll be down for dinner shortly. Go ahead without me," Caroline sang out, hiding her emotions with a cheery tone. She wanted to remain alone and think, but missing dinner would raise all kinds of questions and speculation she had no patience to endure.

No, she would put on a brave face and go down. She would sit across the table and look at Darcy, but she would not be the same hopeful fool she had been earlier in the afternoon when she had brushed her hair and imagined Darcy announcing they were all off to Pemberley.

She was not sure she knew him anymore.

Indeed, she was not sure she understood any man in her life; their motivations were all so foreign to her.

"What to do?" she murmured to herself as she changed for dinner. There was only one answer: they had to vacate Netherfield.

They had to get as far away as possible from Elizabeth Bennet. Louisa would understand the urgency, and she would help. But then, remembering Bingley's ongoing passion for the place, and Darcy's expression of longing while watching Miss Elizabeth sing, she knew it would take more than a simple suggestion on her part to dislodge the party.

It would require a major disruption in their lives and creating this disruption would call for cleverness and no small degree of deception. All of which she was willing to do. Feeling determined and in control, Caroline smoothed her hair, pinched her cheeks, and went to dinner, confident she would prevail.

Her companions spent the meal waxing enthusiastically over the afternoon's guests. Darcy did not even bother to hide his infatuation, she noticed.

"Georgiana, I have one more surprise for you," Darcy said. "I asked Miss Elizabeth to return tomorrow to tutor you on your vocals, as you have long wanted to improve. She has graciously agreed".

"Darcy! That is good news," Georgiana cried out.

"What a shockingly good idea, Darcy," echoed Bingley.

Caroline took a deep breath and said, "Indeed, Miss Elizabeth is a rare find."

"We are in agreement on that," Bingley said to his sister. "I may ask Miss Jane to accompany her. Miss Darcy, you two must meet. I am convinced you will take a great liking to her, as my sisters certainly did."

"I look forward to the introduction to Miss Bennet," Georgiana said. "My, is this the same day that started out so grey and daunting? What a difference our delightful guests made."

"Indeed," Caroline sighed. "To be honest, I find it all very surprising. Mr. Darcy, your interest in music is compelling. Funny how it did not show itself at Pemberley as much as it has here at Netherfield." He was as good as lost to her now, she figured. There was no reason not to dig at him.

"On the contrary," he said with some amusement at her evident annoyance. "Did you forget the beautiful harp that accompanied our afternoons there? Please mark in your ledger that the harp was just one example of the lengths that I will go to in order to indulge in my love of good music, present within me no matter where I reside, be it Pemberley or London or Netherfield."

"That is a very good answer, Mr. Darcy," she complimented him in an attempt to distract from her previous annoyance. "You are correct and have reminded me of a question I have long wished to ask, but which kept slipping my mind. Is there a harp in any residence in Meryton, does anyone recollect?" she said. "If not, the master of Netherfield might inquire into attaining one so Miss Darcy can continue her efforts in that area."

"I know of none," said Mrs. Hurst.

"Nor I," said Bingley. "But procuring a harp is a splendid idea. I will inquire in town when next I go there."

"I fully expect Miss Elizabeth to have several harp solos up her sleeve," Caroline said, looking boldly across the table at Darcy, who did not take her bait.

"Is there anything she is not capable of?" Mrs. Hurst wondered aloud.

# *CHAPTER THIRTEEN*

During the ensuing week of daily visits to Netherfield by Miss Elizabeth, Caroline appeared to be all placid contentment. She moved throughout the days possessing a calm countenance and a ready smile. She made very polite conversation with both Bennet girls when they called, complimenting Jane on her hair comb and forcing herself to sit through the torturous music lessons in order to appear completely unbothered by it all. Caroline always made a point of telling Georgiana that her vocal tone seemed to improve after each lesson

Mr. Darcy regularly popped in to say hello to Miss Elizabeth and observe the lessons. In Caroline's opinion, he overstayed to the point of disruption.

Inwardly, however, her mind was a whirlwind of intrigue. As Miss Elizabeth and Miss Darcy practiced scales, Caroline plotted her escape from Netherfield. Several plans were considered and discarded as too impossible, too impractical, or not an effective enough way to meet her goal of total separation from the place.

Of the few ideas she mulled, only one continued to stand out in her mind. Thinking her plan out thoroughly, she realized that circumstances had already aligned to support her success in the endeavor, should she decide to proceed. By the end of the week, she came to believe that this specific plan, though dangerous, was well worth its inherent risk and would do the necessary job of severing her from Netherfield.

She had endured an excruciating week watching Darcy moon all over Miss Elizabeth. Bingley had behaved like a lapdog to Miss Jane, anticipating her every need and carrying out her wishes as if he were her servant. He was always foisting those ridiculous iced buns on everyone and seeking never-ending praise because of them. Caroline could not endure one more day of his vapid enthusiasm for Meryton or his lovelorn looks at Miss Jane.

How she wished fate had never led him to this wretched place! She wanted out of Netherfield and she wanted out now.

When the last lesson of the week finally ended, and Miss Elizabeth stood up to take her leave, Darcy clearly did not want her to go.

"Please, come again next week. Georgiana is making such progress; can you imagine how much more improvement she will see if you indulge us with another week of lessons?"

Elizabeth readily agreed, as Caroline knew she would. And though Caroline joined everyone in seeing Elizabeth off, calling out their goodbyes until next week, she made up her mind that there would be no second week of lessons at Netherfield.

She had let the ridiculous situation go on too long; that may have been her only error.

It was time to act.

She would do so, that night.

***

Caroline nursed her after-dinner coffee, drinking a second cup of the brew, knowing she would not sleep. She laughed and listened to the drawing room conversation as if she were not possessed by destructive demons.

No one who observed her would ever suspect that she was anything other than tired and sleepy when she joined her sister and Georgiana to retire for the evening. She went through her nightly rituals, washing her face at the basin, combing out her hair, and climbing into the bed.

In her mind, she had set the time of one a.m. as the perfect moment. Her nerves were racing in anticipation and time seemed to drag, but there was no chance that she would sleep. Eventually, the top of the hour arrived, and she rose from her bed automatically, no doubt or fear holding her back. She possessed the same determination as her forefathers—strong men who had built their wealth through grit and a steely will. Men who were not afraid to do what those around them would not do in order to gain an advantage.

She opened the door to her room slowly and peeked her head out in the hall. As expected, it was empty and quiet, and Caroline stepped out of her room and shut the door silently behind her. Stealth was a priority, so she took no candle as she felt her way to the end of the corridor and then down the back staircase until she reached the stairs that led to the kitchen, slowly taking each wide, cold step one at a time. There was no need to rush, she told herself, as there was always plenty of time to hide if she were to hear anyone rustling or approaching.

Yet no one stirred in the household. No one was about to see her and wonder what the fine lady was doing groping about in the dark, her feet bare. When she reached the empty kitchen she worked quickly—positioning the kindling just outside the hearth and then gently scooping a hot ember and transferring it to the dry stuff. She sat crouched on the floor, up close, watching intently as an orange ember licked the kindling, and when the flame began to spread across the kitchen floor, only then did she back away. Slowly, with her eye on the spreading orange glow, she waited until she was doubly sure that the fire had taken hold, and then she scurried, silently and speedily back the way she came, her step light, barely hitting the floorboards. She ascended the stairs quickly and steadily and, in what felt like a mere moment, found herself back in the hallway, quietly opening the door to her room and shutting it behind her with nary a squeak.

Caroline walked to the bed and got in, pulling the coverlet up to her chin, and then she waited, her heart beating rapidly. She laughed softly to herself. With no usable kitchen, Netherfield would be uninhabitable. Darcy would not allow his precious sister to live in such primitive conditions, and he and Miss Darcy would be forced to return to Pemberley. And, generous friend that he was, he would graciously invite her and Bingley and the Hursts, back to Pemberley with him.

She laughed again, imaging the expressions on the Bennet family when they learned that Netherfield Hall caught fire and must be abandoned until spring at the earliest when necessary repairs could start. Mrs. Bennet would fall right over into her soup from shock. She imagined Jane would smile serenely when faced with the news that Bingley had left town, but then she would proceed to move about her day, appearing quite unbothered.

And as for Miss Elizabeth Bennet? If she had designs on Darcy, would she be clever enough to realize that she had been outsmarted?

Caroline listened carefully for the sounds of shouting that she knew would come. She waited patiently, excitedly, until at last, she heard in the distance the first shout of "Fire!" Quickly, she turned on her side with her back to the door and closed her eyes, imitating the posture of someone deeply asleep. Soon she heard the heavy thud of feet moving quickly from room to room, the sound of a fist pounding rapidly at a door, frantic voices, voices raised in alarm, and then it was her turn as footsteps ran toward her room, and then a hurried rap, rap, rap sounded on her door.

Col. Fitzwilliam didn't wait for an answer but burst in.

"Miss Bingley, wake up! Fire downstairs. Come quickly," he said, breathing deeply.

Caroline continued feigning sleep, but at his second entreaty, she shook herself awake and expressed the appropriate alarm. Col. Fitzwilliam's face was red and his hair unkempt; there was real panic in his eyes. Moving quickly, she grabbed a shawl and hurriedly followed him out into the hall where Georgiana and the Hursts could already be seen rushing toward the stairs.

Col. Fitzwilliam directed them, "Fire in the kitchen; you should be safe enough in the west sunroom. Go there and wait."

Mr. Hurst said, "I'll escort the ladies and be right with you."

Col. Fitzwilliam nodded and rushed off.

Once safely ensconced in the sunroom, the three women huddled together in the dark, somber and silent, listening to the sound of yelling and shouting in the distance.

"I wish I could go out there and help," said Georgiana.

"As do I," Caroline assured her, grabbing her hand and squeezing it.

"All we can do is wait and worry," Mrs. Hurst said sleepily.

The minutes passed slowly, until eventually the shouting wound down, and then there was nothing but silence.

Ten minutes or so later, they heard the sound of boots pounding down the corridor toward them, and Darcy burst into the room, bedraggled and wet, his dark hair sticking to his forehead, and his face flushed a deep red from exertion.

"It's all right, now; the fire is out."

"Oh, thank goodness! Is everyone safe?" exclaimed Georgiana anxiously.

"The fire was contained to the kitchen. Thankfully, Col. Fitzwilliam smelled the smoke when he did, or else the whole place might have been burned. But as it is, we were able to put it out before it spread."

"Thank goodness!" Caroline exclaimed. "How frightening! We might all have died. Who was there last in the kitchen?"

"Obviously, one of the staff. We'll question them all in the morning," Darcy said as he wiped his forehead with his handkerchief.

"Whoever it was will never admit it," Mrs. Hurst said, shaking her head.

Darcy shrugged. "It was an accident, most likely. We must be grateful that it was not worse, although the kitchen is now out of commission until we can rebuild. The smoke alone has made it uninhabitable."

"Oh, what are we to do?" cried out Mrs. Hurst. "How will we eat?"

"We can't stay here," exclaimed Georgiana, putting her hand to her mouth in dismay.

"No, we shall have to go home," Darcy said. "It's a pity since you just arrived." Turning to Caroline and Mrs. Hurst, Darcy said, "You ladies must join us, of course, although I am sure Bingley will want to stay put for the time being."

"Oh, yes, thank you, Mr. Darcy, you are too kind for including us. This is dreadful news. What a shame. And what a shock it will be to Bingley. Have you seen him?" Caroline played her part well.

"He is coping as best as possible. He is grateful that the damage was not severe, but as for the future of his lease here, I am uncertain what his liability is and whether or not the owner will cancel the lease."

"Cancel the lease?" Caroline exclaimed. She had not thought of that possibility, which fit her purposes wonderfully.

"Oh, I hope not," exclaimed Georgiana. "Bingley would be devastated."

Darcy nodded. "Yes, he would be. He is quite shaken up. Here, let me escort you all back to the drawing room and out of this cold dark spot. Mr. Hurst was making up the fire and the room should be warming up nicely."

Pulling their shawls and blankets tightly around them, they followed Darcy back down the hallway to the drawing room, where Mr. Hurst had the fire up and roaring. Soon Bingley and Col. Fitzwilliam joined them, breathing heavily, sinking into their seats in exhaustion. Their clothes were damp from tossing water and their clothes smelled of smoke.

"We were able to put it out quickly, but I've never run so hard and so fast in my life," Bingley said.

"Lucky thing that well was close by. But most thanks to the Colonel here for sounding the alarm," Hurst said, mopping his forehead.

"You were not asleep?" Bingley asked of Col. Fitzwilliam.

"Off and on. I was restless all night," he answered. "I just happened to have been awake for some time and was able to smell the smoke immediately. I knew something was wrong and went downstairs not knowing what I would find. Much to my relief, none of the living areas were on fire, but just as I went toward the kitchen the source was obvious. Luckily, the stable man woke too, and he roused the help while I went back upstairs. I first woke Darcy then Bingley, and then stayed back to escort the ladies."

"We are so grateful you were awake," said Georgiana.

"We owe our lives to you," Mrs. Hurst said, shaking her head.

"Yes, what bravery you exhibited," Caroline added. So Col. Fitzwilliam had not been asleep, she thought with some degree of worry. But, she reasoned quickly, as his room was at the far end of the opposite corridor, there could be no way he had heard her or would suspect her involvement. His bedroom window was closest to the kitchen, she estimated, making it logical that he would be the first to smell smoke. She couldn't decide if it were lucky or not that he was awake and there to sound the alarm at the perfect time.

The drawing room door opened again, and in came the cook with trays of steaming hot tea.

"The stable boy made a little fire, and we were able to boil the water up real nice. Here, to take the chill off. Sorry, I have no cakes for you all as they were burnt up in the fire. I am so sorry, Master Bingley. I swear that fire were safely put out like always," she insisted.

"Do not blame yourself," Bingley replied. "These things happen."

"But I can't explain it for the life of me. It makes no sense. None at all," she continued, on the verge of tears. "Did anyone see anything? Anyone inside the kitchen or about the property that shouldn't have been there?"

The group shook their heads no in unison, including Col.

Fitzwilliam, which reassured Caroline greatly.

"We'll get to the bottom of it somehow," Hurst assured her.

"Now get yourself back to bed," Bingley said. "There is nothing more that we need."

"And thank you so much for the tea," Caroline said warmly. "Extraordinary effort on your part, don't we all agree?"

A round of thank-yous poured from the gathered party and, reluctantly, the cook departed. Caroline sat back and drank the steaming tea, warming her hands against its warm sides. She listened with interest as the men discussed what to do next.

"We shouldn't try to do too much tonight. The ladies should go back to bed; there's plenty of time to discuss everything in the morning," Darcy said.

"I hardly think I will sleep," Georgiana said. "Are you sure the fire's completely out? I'm a little frightened."

"The danger is gone, but do not fret. We will be up for a while to keep watch," Darcy assured her.

"Come, Miss Darcy; I'll walk you up," Caroline offered. Reassured, Georgiana joined the ladies and headed back upstairs. Despite the terrible turn of events, soon all three women were sleeping soundly.

# CHAPTER FOURTEEN

Caroline opened her eyes. Sunlight was streaming in at the edges of the drawn draperies. She had slept harder and longer than she imagined she would after her exertions of the previous night. But it had been a brilliant plan, flawlessly executed on her end, and she congratulated herself. No one was hurt, and the kitchen was out of commission for weeks. As she hoped he would, Darcy offered them all sanctuary at Pemberley. She was confident that once Darcy was back at Pemberley, he would forget his flirtation with Miss Elizabeth.

She dressed quickly; no maid appeared to help her, but that was to be expected. She anticipated a very busy day packing and beginning their drive back to Pemberley. Caroline gathered a few possessions together from throughout the room in preparation for taking her leave, and then when she had achieved a satisfactory level of organization, she left to go downstairs. There would be no breakfast in her room this morning. Instead, she headed to the dining room, but it was dark and deserted. However, she could hear voices in the drawing room and headed that way.

Entering the room, she saw that everyone was up and dressed; she was the last one to come downstairs. Joining them were Sir William Lucas and several other men she recognized from the neighborhood, Mr. Bennet among them. A spread of breads and fruits and pastries filled a nearby table. The smell of musky smoke still hung in the air, but she could also smell the aroma of hot coffee.

"Good morning," Caroline said, offering everyone her most serene smile. "What a lovely spread. Wherever did it come from?"

"From our wonderful neighbors. Didn't I tell you they were the best?" Bingley boasted.

"Yes, you did, many times," she said sweetly, feeling that she could afford to be magnanimous as she would not have to endure the company of said lovely neighbors much longer. "Thank you all for your generosity. However did you come to know so quickly of our troubles last night?"

Sir William said, "No thanks are necessary. That's what a tight community does in times of trouble. The help got the word out, and the ladies and cooks insisted that we share our breakfast with the good folks at Netherfield.  No one will go hungry, burnt kitchen or not, on my watch."

Caroline took a hot cup of coffee and balanced it on her saucer. "I'll remember the good people of Meryton with much gratitude whilst we are away."

"But none of us here want you to go away! We were just telling Mr. Darcy here that there is no need to leave town," Sir William said. "We've plenty of room at Lucas Lodge for the ladies to stay with us."

"And plenty of families who will host you all for dinner," added Mr. Bennet.

Caroline assembled a plate for herself and carried it to a nearby chair and sat down. When she was settled, she said, "Thank you so much for the offer; I'm sure we couldn't impose."

But Darcy was nodding his head affirmatively and smiling broadly at Sir William. "You are all truly the best of neighbors. I appreciate your offer more than words can say as I despair at the idea of leaving Bingley in the lurch in his time of need."

"Yes, thank you so much. You are too kind," Georgiana exclaimed, echoing her brother's sentiments. "I feel very strongly that as Bingley will not leave Netherfield, we should not either. Your kind offer makes it possible for us to stay here with him."

Caroline could not believe what she was hearing. Last night Darcy spoke with certainty that they would leave for Pemberley. How did he come to be so easily influenced by the locals into changing his mind? His inconstancy was as alarming as the plan forming in front of her. This turnabout had to be the Bennets' influence. Of course, they would not let Darcy out of their sights, but how could he be so foolish as to be taken in by them?

Did he not see, as she did, how they would not let him go?

She felt the teacup rattling on the saucer as her hand began to tremble. She set it down quickly before anyone noticed.

"I cannot help but feel that this would be an enormous imposition on everyone involved," Caroline persisted. At last, her composure failed and tears of disappointment began streaming down her face.

Darcy was quick to hand her his handkerchief. She dabbed

her eyes as the room's occupants looked at her with true sympathy.

"There, there, Miss Bingley. Do not cry," said Sir William from across the room.

"She is sensitive," Bingley said lovingly, and he came to her side and began to gently stroke her hair, which irritated Caroline immensely. Yet she knew with all the room's attention upon her, she could not shake her brother off.

"Sir William has plenty of room," Bingley went on in a soothing manner. "You need not worry about enduring several days of an unnecessary journey back to Derbyshire when you are already so upset and exhausted."

"I am not used to such kindness," Caroline lied through her tears, feeling cornered and outnumbered. She dabbed her eyes and flashed a weak smile to the room.

"Eat something," said Mrs. Hurst. "You'll feel better."

Nodding, Caroline broke off a piece of bread and butter and slowly chewed. "I'm fine, thank you all."

The conversation then turned to the topic of the renovation. As she sat and ate, Caroline looked about the room at her companions. Inexplicably, all of them would rather remain where they were and impose on the hospitality of others than retreat to a perfectly luxurious estate where they could resume some sense of normal life. Darcy and Bingley were chatting animatedly with the men as if they hadn't been torn from their beds and up all night. She glanced at Col. Fitzwilliam, who was staring at her with a strange expression on his face that made her uneasy, and she looked away.

It appeared that staying in Meryton was a *fait accompli*.

"Be assured that every night, some family will be ready to provide dinner and company," said one of the villagers whose name Caroline could not recall.

"You will all dine at Longbourn with us tomorrow night," Mr. Bennet added.

A series of revolving dinners with all the commonfolk in Meryton?

It was the stuff of nightmares.

Caroline put down the bread and butter as she was beginning to feel sick.

"Not to worry, Bingley. We will get this burnt kitchen cleared out and a new one built up for you in no time," said Sir William. "Why, it will be better than ever."

Bingley looked from face to face with gratitude. "I cannot thank you enough. I always knew that Meryton was a special place, and this horrible incident has proved me right."

Sir William addressed the women, "I will have my coach come for you at half-past eleven. That way, you will be at Lucas Lodge in time for luncheon."

Georgiana teared up in gratitude. "Thank you so much. How happy I will be to see Miss Charlotte again."

"She has a younger sister, Maria, who will be so pleased for your company as well," he added.

"Then we mustn't waste any time," Caroline said, thankful for a reason to excuse herself. "There is much preparation to be made." She looked at her brother. "Send the staff up to our rooms as soon as possible."

Bingley nodded in agreement. "I'll go inform them."

He joined step with his sister as they made their way out of the room. "You will be well-taken care of, Caroline. Be thankful it wasn't worse," he said, as he held the door open for her.

"Yes, that goes without saying," she snapped at him. Then recovering, she said quickly, "I'm sorry. The upset and lack of sleep have left me a little short-tempered. Do forgive me."

Bingley was always all forgiveness to his sister. "It will only be an inconvenience for about a fortnight; maybe a little longer. Then we will all be back together here. I suspect you'll enjoy yourself very much with the Lucas family."

"Yes," Caroline nodded, feeling dead and defeated.

The women returned to their rooms where the staff soon joined them to help organize and pack. Caroline moved through the motions numbly, aghast at the turn of events that now saw her not only lodging with the Lucas family but thrust into the heart of Meryton society every night for who knew how long.

This time, there were no other options. No chance to think what to do next. Maintaining her composure in an unfamiliar home would require all of her energy. Not to mention the tremendous acting job she would now have to perform whenever they discussed the fire. Pretending that she cared about the destruction of Netherfield was taxing; she expected that keeping up the façade would get very dull very quickly. But she couldn't let down her guard for an instant. Col. Fitzwilliam had looked at her in such a way that she had almost imagined he knew her secret.

But he couldn't.

Could he?

She shook off that idea. From all the talk, it was apparent that no one had seen her, and no one suspected her. And who would ever accuse a lady like her of such a deed?

Presently, she was packed and dressed and waiting in the drawing room with Mrs. Hurst and Miss Darcy for the Lucas coach to arrive. The menfolk had scattered, and the ladies were fatigued and did not engage in much conversation. Caroline was thankful for that.

The carriage came on time, and soon the ladies were deposited at the door of Lucas Lodge. Their accommodations were surprisingly comfortable and elegant, for Meryton, Caroline thought, and she welcomed the chance to share a room again with her sister. Miss Darcy's room was situated across the hall and was just as comfortable, albeit a bit smaller, which pleased Caroline for some reason.

At luncheon, the conversation revolved, unsurprisingly, around the events of the fire. Caroline put on her best performance, describing the night's events in a serious tone, expressing her gratitude that it was not worse, and praising the people of Meryton for their charity.

"However did it start?" wondered Lady Lucas.

Mrs. Hurst said, "We do not have confirmation, but one of our servant girls is very sloppy. Although she will never admit it, my suspicions reside there. I suspect Miss Lilly."

Caroline remained calm, but inside she rejoiced at how easily her sister pointed the finger exactly where Caroline wanted. "Miss Lilly? Really?" Caroline exclaimed, displaying incredulity best she could.

"Then you must let her go," Lady Lucas said firmly.

"Oh, Bingley would never hear of it. In fact, please do not mention my sister's suspicions to him. It will upset him so," Caroline urged sweetly. "Everyone has trouble with staff."

"I promise not to say anything to Bingley, but how can you sleep at night knowing she might make the same mistake again, and this time you might all suffocate from smoke whilst you sleep! No, you must take it up with her to make sure it never happens again," Lady Lucas warned.

"I pray that such an event will not occur twice. May I assure you that I will have a firm word with this young lady so that she is too frightened to make the same mistake," Caroline said, certain that she had struck the right mixture of innocence and concern.

The men joined them at dinner, and Caroline was content to sit back and listen as they each relayed their own stories of waking up and extinguishing the fire. She was adroit at anticipating and mimicking the company's reactions, and was thus alternately wide-eyed, then amazed, then astonished at their tales of smelling smoke and waking the staff and working the well and running with the pails of water and so on and so on.

Will every meal in Meryton be accompanied by the

excruciatingly detailed retelling of this same story, she wondered? She imagined it to be so and regretted the dull, dull evenings ahead of her.

Nevertheless, she played her part brilliantly, although she was cognizant that Col. Fitzwilliam's gaze seemed to land on her often whenever she spoke about that evening. Strategically, she took to smiling back at him in return, almost like a little game, daring him to think her disingenuous or guilty in some way. Surely, someone with something to hide could not stomach such intense scrutiny nor look their accuser in the eye and smile so casually?

After dinner, there was a call for music. Charlotte attended to the pianoforte and began to play. Caroline noticed with a sinking feeling that Darcy paid scant attention to the performance, looking around the room distractedly. He clapped half-heartedly when she was finished and made no call for an encore, and this only added to Caroline's misery.

# CHAPTER FIFTEEN

Predictably, Darcy's enthusiasm for musical performance resumed the next evening when they dined as the guests of the Bennets. Caroline dreaded going; she was tempted to call off with a headache but decided that she could not quit her vigil where Darcy and Miss Elizabeth were concerned.

As was the case the previous evening, upon gathering in the Bennet's drawing room, the conversation centered on the events of the fire and the hours afterward. Caroline was grateful for the pause that ensued as the group moved into the dining room.

They sat down to dinner at a very cramped table. Mrs. Bennet strategically placed Darcy at the foot of the table with Elizabeth and Jane at either side. Bingley was next to Jane, of course, and the four seemed always to have their heads together as they engaged in a high-spirited conversation.

Mrs. Bennet hedged her bets that Col. Fitzwilliam might be a worthy suitor for one of her daughters and so placed him between Lydia and Kitty. Mr. Bennet and Mr. Hurst sat together and immediately fell into a tiresome conversation about bull breeding. Caroline, Mrs. Hurst and Miss Darcy were seated together at the opposite end of the table to be interrogated further by Mrs. Bennet and Mary.

"I've never been evacuated myself, but I oftentimes imagine how I would react if I were to be roused out of bed in the middle of the night," Mrs. Bennet said. "I would grab my pearls and my emerald comb before running out."

"As did I," Mrs. Hurst said. "I was certain that the whole of Netherfield was to go up in flames, so I ran for my diamond brooch, despite Col. Fitzwilliam's insistence that I hurry."

"Miss Darcy, did you have the presence of mind to take any special possession?" Mary asked.

"Yes, I too thought the place would be lost completely and took a moment to procure my mother of pearl hairbrush and mirror set that my aunt had just given me new, and my garnet earrings from the tray on the table. Most of my precious items were thankfully back at Pemberley," Georgiana said.

"And you, Miss Bingley. What did you take in the rush?" Mrs. Bennet asked.

Caroline had been so busy pretending to be asleep and then acting surprised that she had not thought she should also try to save her possessions. That was a mistake, she thought to herself, but hopefully Col. Fitzwilliam took no notice in the moment. She quickly debated whether she should make up a story; it was only Mrs. Bennet asking, after all, and no one ever listened to her nonsense. But she decided not to fabricate details that could be disproved later.

"No, I did not take any jewelry or items. My head was foggy from being so harshly awakened that I couldn't think." She smiled boldly across the table at Mrs. Bennet. "Luckily, I did not lose anything precious, although I brought scant valuables with me as I purposely left my nice things in London."

"That was a smart move," Mary said. "As I find I inexplicably lose possessions in the packing and unpacking process, or from the upset of my possessions being under the care of a strange lady's maid."

"I heard Mr. Darcy was all set to decamp back to Pemberley until Sir William stepped in," Mrs. Bennet said. "Thank God for Sir William! We are all most grateful to him, as the regiment has moved on, and we were facing a very dull time staring at the same faces."

Mrs. Bennet looked down the table at her daughters and tried to catch their attention with a wave. Unable to distract them, she sighed and turned back to her current companions. "From the looks of it, it appears that Mr. Bingley and Mr. Darcy are enjoying the evening very much."

Georgiana observed her brother's animated spirits, and a smile lit up her face. "Yes, my brother seems to be won over by the Meryton society as much as Mr. Bingley. I am glad for their sake that they did not have to be parted. My brother is fiercely protective of me, and his first instinct was to get me back home to Pemberley. But he is also fiercely loyal to his friends. I could tell he was relieved he did not have to abandon Bingley in his hour of need. My brother is quite capable in matters of building and managing staff, and he will be an asset to the restoration project."

"Mr. Darcy must have tremendous experience managing a

place such as Pemberley. I hear it is elegance and charm in perfect proportion," Mrs. Bennet said.

Georgiana, too naïve to detect Mrs. Bennet's self-serving curiosity, thanked her for the compliment. "To me, it is home, but my brother deeply feels his responsibility to be the best master of Pemberley. So many of our staff have been in service with us since my father and mother were alive, and he will not let them down."

"I've heard you can buy a ticket and tour it," said Mary. "My, how I would love to live in a place that sold tickets to tour."

"How many rooms, did you say?" Mrs. Bennet went on.

Georgiana paused thoughtfully, trying to add them up. "I know there are at least thirty rooms."

"I imagine they are all finely furnished?" Mary said. "And is there a library? That is where I would lose myself."

"Yes, a wonderful library," Georgiana said, describing the interior with affection until Mrs. Bennet became bored with the topic of books and was anxious to move the party on from the dinner table.

"Lizzy, the pianoforte, now," she commanded when they all gathered in the drawing room. When Elizabeth was slow to move, Mary Bennet commandeered the instrument. She then subjected the company to three of her favorite musical pieces. To everyone's relief, only one had a vocal component.

"That's enough, Mary, or you'll ruin the evening for everyone," Mrs. Bennet yelled across the room. She glanced over at Elizabeth with a look of impatience. Mary bowed, and Elizabeth reluctantly rose and took her place.

Elizabeth also performed three pieces, and again, Darcy's gaze was fixed on her as if he were in a trance. After studying Darcy for an excruciatingly painful minute, Caroline looked away in disgust, only to accidentally meet the gaze of Col. Fitzwilliam as she did so. Tired of life's disappointments, Caroline did not bother to mask her pain.

She was past caring how many of her secrets Col. Fitzwilliam guessed.

Col. Fitzwilliam did not insult her by smiling at her or requiring one in return. He, too, saw that Fitzwilliam Darcy had fallen for Miss Elizabeth Bennet. It might take Darcy months to admit it, but those most familiar with the man saw the light in his eyes and the drastic change that came over him when in Miss Elizabeth's presence.

Caroline glanced at the timepiece on the mantle, estimating the number of minutes in the evening she was required to endure before experiencing the sweet relief of departing. Like the gentleman that he was, Col. Fitzwilliam arrived at her side and stayed there for the remainder of the evening, refusing to let her be alone.

When at last Caroline was settled into bed, she vowed to have a headache for the next night's dinner, scheduled to be held at the home of Mr. and Mrs. Phillips. The Bennet family was included, of course. No relative of Mrs. Bennet would be allowed to entertain Mr. Darcy and Mr. Bingley without the presence of Miss Jane or Miss Elizabeth.

She decided that the first thing she would do the next morning would be to ask Louisa to write to the staff at their London home to prepare for their return.

"I don't know why I didn't think of that myself," Mrs. Hurst said the next morning as they discussed the idea in their shared room. "I must have been operating under a mistaken belief that our presence was needed to support Bingley, but the reality is that we have done nothing but be a burden to the community here."

"My thoughts exactly," Caroline said. "Why be indebted to these fine people when we are not homeless? Let them have their spare rooms and their dining tables back to themselves. I cannot impinge on their generosity any longer."

"So you are abandoning all hope for Darcy?" Mrs. Hurst gazed tenderly at her sister.

Caroline sighed. "He is insufferable around Miss Elizabeth. Don't you agree?"

"He is quite transparent in his interest. Everyone notices. I am so sorry."

"He may do whatever he wishes, but I will not stand by and watch the poor man embarrass himself with such a common woman. Perhaps it's time I start over in London, this new season, and get away from this miserable county," Caroline declared.

"Good decision. But you must promise me that you will try harder than you did last season. You left the clear impression that Darcy was the only man for you despite me warning you it was a bad look."

"Perhaps I did, but I did not pass up a more suitable suitor at the same time, did I? No loss there."

"Shall we ask Miss Darcy to return with us?" Mrs. Hurst wondered. "Darcy would most likely come to procure her."

"True. Let us extend an invitation and see if she accepts," Caroline agreed, her spirits rising at the thought of being in London by the end of the week.

"I will ask Mr. Hurst this morning," Mrs. Hurst promised.

But when Mrs. Hurst broached the subject of returning to London, Mr. Hurst sadly refused his wife's request. Mrs. Hurst called Caroline back to the privacy of their room to deliver the news.

"Mr. Hurst says no. He can't spare the carriage and insists it is bad form to abandon Bingley. It will look like we are inconstant during times of trouble and he won't do it," Mrs. Hurst said. "He wants us to be here for Bingley when the place is restored."

Caroline scowled with annoyance. "What a shame. As for Mr. Hurst's sense of loyalty, may I say I am surprised? I didn't think he had it in him."

"Me neither."

"But did you tell him we are making ourselves a burden to the local folk? He would not want to be indebted."

"I impressed that fact upon him, but he assured me that to leave on that account would be a greater insult to the people of Meryton. He insists we must accept the hospitality as offered," Mrs. Hurst replied. "I'm sorry. I too, prefer to return."

Caroline turned away. She had gone from the fire to the

frying pan, she thought and wanted out as quickly as she could.

As Mr. Hurst repeated everything to anyone who would listen, word of the women's fear that they were a burden circulated in the Lucas household and in the neighborhood. The Lucas family immediately reassured Caroline and Mrs. Hurst that such fears were ungrounded. The men took their sentiments to heart and vowed to work as fast as their fingers would let them to restore Netherfield so the women could return.

Caroline was so disheartened by this news that she decided to have a headache. By late afternoon, she reported being too ill to leave her room.

"You all go ahead to the Phillips' for dinner. I will stay back so as not to spoil the evening," Caroline said apologetically.

"Nonsense," said Georgiana. "I could not enjoy myself knowing that you were not with us."

"Miss Charlotte and Miss Maria are here. And besides, depending how my headache progresses, I may not be up for company," Caroline protested. Despite their pleas, Caroline insisted they not disappoint the Phillips. "Mr. and Mrs. Phillips have most likely made many preparations for the evening." Georgiana reluctantly consented to leave Caroline behind.

Tired of everyone, Caroline retreated to her dark room, refusing to have any candles lit, only a small fire. There she waited, wide awake, until she heard the sound of the doors slamming and the carriage pulling away to the Phillips.

Miraculously, Caroline's symptoms lifted less than an hour

later, and she was able to join the Lucas family, who were eager to pamper her. Caroline accepted their ministrations and was soon so recovered that she won two rounds of whist, which was a balm to her competitive spirit. Lady Lucas offered to read aloud, and Caroline much enjoyed the soothing tones of her genteel voice. She was very grateful for the quiet evening at Lucas Lodge, far away from yet another musical performance by the Bennet sisters.

***

"Yes, she did sing again, and he was just as transparent in his delight," Mrs. Hurst whispered to Caroline as they sat alone in the drawing room after breakfast the next morning. "You didn't really have a headache, did you?" she added.

"No, of course not. I never get ill," Caroline whispered back. "I simply cannot stomach watching Miss Elizabeth Bennet's coy performance. She is reeling Darcy in like a fat bass, and he is oblivious to her bait."

"Yes, it appears so."

"How was the Phillips home? Very drab?"

"The furnishings and rooms were mediocre, but her cook was good—the pastries were sublime. But you would not be sorry to have missed it."

"It will be Christmastide soon. Will Darcy stay in Meryton, do you think?"

"I have not heard otherwise. Oh, good morning, Bingley,"

Mrs. Hurst greeted her brother.

"Good morning. Checking up on my sister to make sure she is feeling better." He looked at Caroline sympathetically.

"Much better, thank you. Staying back and avoiding the evening air seemed to make all the difference," Caroline lied.

"We were just mentioning that Christmas will be here in a few weeks. Does Darcy plan to return to Pemberley?" Mrs. Hurst inquired.

"I can say with certainty that he does not," Bingley announced with a wide grin. "In fact, we both feel under a great deal of obligation for the generosity we have been the recipients of during this ordeal. And I was thinking, when the kitchen is finished, what better way to break it in than to throw open the doors of Netherfield for a grand holiday party?"

"Another ball? Charles, are you insane?" Caroline asked.

"No, no," he said quickly. "Not a ball—the Meryton Christmas assembly is already a village tradition. Instead, what I propose is a friendly dinner to repay all those who hosted us. The Lucases, the Bennets, the Phillips and all the men and their families who donated their time to rebuild Netherfield."

"That sounds like a crowd," Caroline said, but she eventually agreed that the party was a necessary gesture in light of all the hospitality they had received. "How soon do the men think it will be until the kitchen is finished?"

"They are telling me the end of next week, if the weather holds out. I feel so blessed that the owner commissioned the modernization. He seemed almost sheepish in telling me it was well overdue."

"Next week! It will be nice to get back to Netherfield; I rather miss it," Mrs. Hurst said.

"This dinner you are suggesting will take a great deal of work and organization. I simply don't know if I am up to it," Caroline confessed.

"My sentiments exactly," echoed Mrs. Hurst.

"But I cannot do it alone," Bingley protested. "Please, Darcy has promised to help. Do say you will do it. I am dependent on your help."

Caroline thought that she would rather jump from a window than host another evening where she would be forced to watch Darcy stare at Miss Elizabeth. Still, in Bingley's earnest desire she saw an opening—a plan much easier than setting another room on fire.

"Very well, I can never refuse you," she said. "I will do it as a favor. Make no mistake, I am grateful for the hospitality extended to me, especially from Sir William and Lady Lucas. But may I ask one thing from you in return for my efforts?"

"Anything," Bingley said, delighted at her concession.

"I do desire a change of scene. These country winters are so dull. Let us throw the party but then return to London for a month or two of city pleasures."

"But … no … but why?" Bingley stammered, and his expression was one of pure disappointment. No matter how much he wished it, his sister had not fallen under the spell of Meryton and refused to be happy there.

Noting his reluctance, Caroline frowned and said, "Bingley, you gave me your word I could have anything. You will have done enough for these folks. Now it is time you do something for me. I do not intend to miss the entire season sitting in Hertfordshire stitching by the fire."

"Your sister is right," Mrs. Hurst said. "It is time you thought of her future. There is nothing for her here. Let us spend a few months in London. The people of Hertfordshire will be here, frozen in place, I imagine, by the time of the spring thaw."

"Very well," Bingley acquiesced. "I may not always be the most thoughtful brother, but I do care about your future," he said to Caroline. "And as for there being nothing for you in Hertfordshire, I believe you are sadly mistaken," he said.

Thus agreed on the compromise—the party in exchange for a return to London, the three spent the next half of an hour planning before Bingley rode back to Netherfield.

"A very clever bargain," Mrs. Hurst complimented her sister. "But we must still endure another evening of the Bennets."

"Remind me to cut the strings of the pianoforte the afternoon of," Caroline said with a roll of her eyes.

# *CHAPTER SIXTEEN*

The autumn weather held out. The roads were clear and the days dry, making supplies and labor easy to procure. Bingley was very encouraged, and he collected the ladies from Lucas Lodge and brought them to Netherfield to take a peek at the progress. The smell of new lumber filled the air as Bingley marched them about the site, pointing out the improvements. Georgiana was delighted, Mrs. Hurst had never stepped into the original kitchen and thus had nothing to compare, and Caroline feigned astonishment as Bingley rambled on about the improvements.

Little does Bingley know he can credit me, she laughed to herself.

Three days later, the project was declared finished and the carriages sent to Lucas Lodge to collect the trio and bring them back home. They settled in quickly, as there was much to do to prepare the home for the upcoming dinner of gratitude and the advent of the holidays.

During the festive season, Caroline always oversaw the trimming of the doors and mantels with greenery, and she did the same at Netherfield. She recruited Bingley and Col. Fitzwilliam to measure the doorframes and mantels and aid in sourcing the decorations from the spruce plot on the property.

Bingley and Col Fitzwilliam managed the wagon as they gathered evergreen boughs and branches, sprigs of mistletoe, and buckets of pinecones. They worked tirelessly for the better part of an hour until Caroline thought they had enough greenery to string together. Upon returning home, they spread their haul across the front steps of Netherfield. Col. Fitzwilliam ran to get the string and scissors that Caroline needed. They tied the boughs together forming a lengthy strand of garland that would perfectly frame the drawing room doorway. When Bingley was called away, Col. Fitzwilliam and Caroline continued working steadily.

They laid the mistletoe in a shady spot on the steps to dry out in anticipation of being fashioned into a ball and hung from the center of the garland.

"It's a shame that this happy time together at Netherfield will be coming to an end in the New Year," Col. Fitzwilliam said casually as they worked the string around the branches.

"Yes, a shame, but country winters are not for me," Caroline said gaily.

"If it were a Derbyshire winter, would that make a difference?" he inquired.

"Of course not," Caroline said. "All the trees and roads and valleys look the same to me, whether in Hertfordshire or Derbyshire. I am an unattached woman, and I crave London and its society."

"As a second son who must also find a wife, I too, find myself reluctantly heading to London every year."

Caroline was surprised to hear his response but kept her focus on threading the boughs together and said, "Surely a man from Darcy's family line has plenty of options when choosing a spouse? Some distant cousin or pretty young neighbor?"

"One might expect such, but that is not the case. I am not the eldest son. Though I wish to marry for love, I will not inherit as my brother will. I do not feel as free as Darcy to be captivated by a woman based on her personality, be it intelligence, strength, or discipline, the particular traits I find myself drawn to."

"Or singing ability," she quipped. He chuckled at her response, and after a moment's pause, he said, "Nevertheless, I prefer to be at Pemberley with my cousins as much as possible. Like you, I am happiest in Derbyshire. But when I marry, should my wife have money, then I may be forced to live where she is happiest, and it may be in a more distant part of the country."

"So you put off forming an attachment to stay close to Darcy and Miss Darcy," Caroline said.

"Yes. And to be able to spend time freely at Pemberley. Is that wrong of me?"

"I don't think so."

"Me, neither. But there is also something new. My brother has surprisingly been somewhat unwell as of late and has of yet no male heir, so now I must choose as if I may one day inherit Blackstone, the family home. It is tricky as my future can go two very different directions."

"I am sure that your search for a spouse will go your way,

but you are wise to think ahead. I try to do so as much as possible," she declared.

"Then we are of similar minds," he said. She glanced over at him to better understand his meaning, but he did not meet her gaze and instead was focused entirely on the task at hand. They worked silently together until Col. Fitzwilliam said, "If I may be allowed to say so, there is one thing that stands out about you to me, more than any other young lady I've met."

"What is that?"

"When I was required to rouse the party from their sleep the night of the fire, it did not go unnoticed by me that you did not run to grab a necklace or a brooch or a special comb, but came with me immediately, with no regard for losing your personal possessions."

Burnt crumpets!

How he tormented her by bringing up that night!

It was not a topic she cared to dwell on with him, but she had plenty of practice maintaining a calm composure where the topic of the Netherfield fire was concerned, and so she remained unruffled.

"That is true," she said guardedly. "I did not think to grab any trinkets or jewelry. How very observant."

Col. Fitzwilliam nodded and continued. "And I thought to myself, now there is a young woman who did not put a prized possession ahead of her own life. It is commendable."

"Why thank you," she said, slightly relieved at his refreshing take on her performance. "You are most kind."

"You know that the other ladies were very concerned and

went about grabbing this or that before I could urge them out of their rooms. To be honest, occasionally I did wonder why your behavior veered so markedly from that of the other young ladies. The thought did cross my mind that perhaps if one knew that the fire was a small one or confined to an enclosed area separate from your room, one would be content to leave their precious things where they were, knowing they were safe."

Caroline could feel her heart skip a beat at his statement. She kept her eyes down and her hand's rhythm steady as she wrapped the string around the branches.

"What an odd statement to make," she exclaimed. "Really, Col. Fitzwilliam, how would I know the source of the fire? My goodness, I did not even know there was a fire until you rudely burst into an unchaperoned lady's chamber without knocking. I was embarrassed for you to see me in my nightclothes; it felt improper and immodest," she said, hoping to embarrass him so that he never broached the subject again.

"For that I heartily apologize. It could not be helped, and I did avert my eyes."

Caroline saw his face color in embarrassment and was pleased. She said, "Let me assure you, I was in full possession of my wits. I respect fire and know that its course is unpredictable. My first thought was not for my possessions, which I can afford to replace, but for my life, which I hold precious."

"That is exactly what I thought," he said, but Caroline was not sure if he could be believed and so was not ready to let the subject drop without providing him a little more assurance.

"Col. Fitzwilliam, I will not ask you why you chose to share that thought with me now. But I desire to say something more about the situation, if you promise not to hold it against me, for it may not reflect well on me, and I am selfish enough to admit that I like hearing that you think well of me."

"Go on," he said gently.

She lowered her voice so she would not be overhead through an open window. "I had no nice things to grab because I brought no nice bits or bobs with me to Hertfordshire. You see, I desperately wanted Bingley to rent Chipperton in Derbyshire, a lovely old home three miles from the gates of Pemberley. There we could continue in the society in which we were comfortable and familiar. Bingley disappointed me greatly by snapping up Netherfield without giving me the privilege of even seeing it first. Darcy, too, was disappointed that Bingley went his own way.

"I deeply resented Bingley's actions and being required to reside here with him. So perhaps I have been slow to accept this place as home and these neighbors as true friends but were you in my position, beholden to my brother's whims, his comings and his goings, then you might understand my unhappiness. Think of me what you may, but I didn't bring anything nice with me because I was never planning to stay here."

She had finished with her garland, and her fingers were red and cold from work. She rubbed them together for warmth then stood up, taking a quick look at Col. Fitzwilliam. Her words seemed to have quieted his doubts. Pleased that she had dealt with the matter effectively, she said cheerfully, "That's it for the garland; be a dear and bring it inside for me?"

"Why, of course," Col. Fitzwilliam nodded, coiling it together. "My apologies; I did not mean to give offense."

Caroline waved him away. "It was an honest question and I have nothing to hide."

"Forgive me if I say one more thing."

"What?"

"It is not a crime to be unhappy or to want things to be different."

"No, I guess not, although sometimes it feels that way. Here, let me get the door for you."

She pulled open the heavy front entry door, holding it back as Col. Fitzwilliam walked inside with the garland, and she followed him in.

Unwilling to end his time with Caroline, he said, "Now, I would be greatly appreciative for your guidance as to how you want this hung."

"Gladly," she responded, feeling a similar desire to continue their easy company. A ladder, and a hammer and nails were procured, and the placing and attaching of the garland absorbed their attention for the next half an hour. They separated when the task was completed; Caroline feeling that the morning had played out surprisingly. Not only had she successfully diverted Col. Fitzwilliam's suspicions, but if she were not mistaken, he had purposely described his prospects in a most attractive way.

She kept her distance from him for the remainder of the day, but thoughts of him occupied her mind. He was no Darcy in stature or wealth and diverting her energy toward a match with Col. Fitzwilliam was never an option when Fitzwilliam Darcy was unattached. But, if the events of the last few weeks had taught her anything, it was that Darcy's attentions to Elizabeth were not waning. And, what was worse, they were evident to everyone.

The door to becoming the mistress of Pemberley seemed to be closing quickly, and Darcy's rejection of her as a possible spouse would sting. Without a backup, tongues would wag. She might find herself the object of pity, or worse, ridicule. However, as Col. Fitzwilliam's spouse, she would be imminently respectable, and she would retain all the benefits of being an insider in Darcy's circle. Should life be as unpredictable as Col. Fitzwilliam wisely pointed out, perhaps he would be in line to inherit Blackstone one day.

These were a set of advantages she owed it to herself to consider. But there would be no rash transference of her interests to Col. Fitzwilliam, if that was his intention in speaking to her.

She needed one more evening observing Darcy and Elizabeth before giving him up for lost.

***

The day of the dinner soon arrived, and the rooms and halls of Netherfield were a whirl of preparation. All the invited guests had accepted the invitation with haste and delight. Bingley opened his purse and spent liberally on meats and sweets and libations and lit the place with twice as many candles as necessary. He fussed about the place, greatly testing the nerves of Caroline and the Hursts.

"My goodness, Bingley. These are the same folks you dined with every day last week. Anything you do for them will be appreciated," Caroline complained.

"Dear boy, take a swig of something to calm yourself," Mr. Hurst advised, calling for Miss Hanna.

"I want everything to be just right. I am so grateful," Bingley insisted. The nip of whiskey calmed him, and he paced around happily for the rest of the day until the festivities began.

Caroline played the gracious hostess alongside Bingley, welcoming the guests and thanking them profusely for their generosity and hospitality in the dark days after the fire displaced them. Her eyes, however, were always focused elsewhere; namely, wherever Darcy happened to be at that moment.

Col. Fitzwilliam hovered around Caroline politely, which annoyed her. However, that annoyance passed as soon as Sir William Lucas approached and provided them with some very interesting news.

"I was in town this afternoon and heard that old man Morrison's barn suffered the same fate as Netherfield," he said with a worrying sigh. "I pray this will not be a pattern."

"Whatever are you referring to?" Caroline inquired, glancing quickly at Col. Fitzwilliam, who seemed equally uninformed.

"There was a small fire in his hay barn at sunrise last week. No idea how it started. Luckily, it too was noticed and put out quickly."

"Goodness, no!" Caroline said, feeling her ears burn.

"You don't know Morrison, he lives ten miles out, but the consensus is that it must have been the same vagabond that got into Netherfield," Sir William asserted. Caroline stole another look at Col. Fitzwilliam, who seemed to be wearing an expression of surprise and great relief.

She wanted to pinch herself; she could not believe her good fortune.

A vagabond was an even better suspect than Miss Lilly!

Ever cognizant of what was required of her in the moment, she composed her face in an appropriate expression of shock and distress. Likewise, Col. Fitzwilliam's expression of suspected relief turned into one of true concern as he considered the damage this vagabond was wreaking on the countryside.

"Is the barn salvageable?" he wondered in a serious tone.

"It's cheaper in these cases to tear it down and start all over," Sir William replied, and the two men delved into a detailed discussion of foundations and support beams and joists.

Meanwhile, Caroline stood by silently, feigning concern whilst all the while dancing inside. Whoever this vagabond was, she felt extremely thankful that his simple attempt to warm himself had served her own purposes so conveniently.

Occasionally, Col. Fitzwilliam would look at her and nod as

he continued his conversation with Sir William. His manner toward her seemed so uplifted that Caroline took it as confirmation that he had been battling his suspicions all along and was now delighted to be relieved of them.

Thus, she did not mind when Col. Fitzwilliam managed to position himself next to her when they sat down to dine. She no longer felt required to keep her guard up around him. He chatted most amiably with her and she flirted back a little at her former silent accuser. Caroline noted with interest that Lady Lucas strategically sat herself on one side of Elizabeth and put her daughter Maria on the other, thus forcing Mr. Darcy into the conveniently empty chair next to Charlotte Lucas.

"Mr. Darcy, do sit here with us next to Miss Charlotte," Lady Lucas exclaimed. Darcy, feeling the weight of the gratitude he owed them for their good care of Georgiana, felt obliged to do as they wished. It cheered Caroline to see that there were other, equally as manipulative forces in Meryton that won out from time to time.

Seated very near to Caroline was Mrs. Bennet, who glared across the table at Lady Lucas. As a sort of retaliation for seating Darcy with Charlotte, Mrs. Bennet spoke loudly and animatedly throughout the courses on her hopes for Jane and Bingley.

Mrs. Bennet loudly itemized the improvements that she thought Jane should make to Netherfield. First off being a change of the wallpaper and window hangings in the very dreary dining room in which they all sat. Caroline listened attentively, her ire growing at the idea of becoming related, albeit distantly, to this woman. Darcy, she was certain, could hear the conversation and would be equally distressed.

Surely he must come to his senses regarding his flirtation with Miss Elizabeth and the wisdom of forming a connection with such a family!

After dinner, they split up to play cards. Caroline found herself seated at a table adjacent to where Darcy and Elizabeth, and Bingley and Jane sat. While waiting her turn, she could not help but listen to the exchange between Darcy and Elizabeth with mounting disgust.

"All Miss Elizabeth does is spar with Darcy. She teases him repeatedly and withholds flattery when he presents a good hand. Surely, she cannot have designs on this man and speak to him so impertinently," she whispered to Mrs. Hurst during a break from the table. Caroline convinced herself that the Darcy she knew was seething inside at the impertinence.

As the night progressed, the voices grew louder, and the group's attention became focused on the mistletoe ball hanging over the doorframe. Caroline noticed with disdain how the young Bennet sisters positioned themselves near the doorway with no hope of being rewarded.

By the time the evening drew to a close, Caroline breathed a sigh of relief. Save for Miss Jane, who was always a sweet and amiable creature, the rest of the Bennets were just as badly behaved as Caroline expected. Lydia and Kitty ran around the rooms squealing, Mary bored everyone she came in contact with by describing the academic tome she was reading, and Caroline saw first-hand the obnoxious and teasing way in which Miss Elizabeth dared speak to Darcy. She was sure that Darcy's disappointment would be severe.

Mrs. Bennet even had the nerve to employ her time-worn trick to delay calling for her carriage so that her girls could mill around on the steps outside and attempt to gain an advantage by being the last to depart. Caroline could not imagine what Mrs. Bennet hoped to achieve by this routine.

As she had already said her goodbyes, Caroline positioned herself in a small hallway leading away from the entry hall and waited alone for the Bennets to leave. Caroline detested the long, drawn-out farewells and adjusting of gloves and winding of scarves that were Mrs. Bennet's way of stalling.

In hanging back, it gave the impression that the entry hall adjacent to the drawing room was empty. Thus hidden, Caroline watched with dread as she saw Darcy and Miss Elizabeth emerge from the drawing room together in quiet conversation. They stopped just under the doorway and time seemed to stand still as she saw Darcy cup Elizabeth's elbow with his hand, draw her close, and tenderly kiss her under the mistletoe. Elizabeth did not blush at the advance but gazed adoringly into Darcy's eyes, which were smiling back at her with great admiration.

Then, furtively, they both glanced around the hallway. Convinced that they were alone, Darcy kissed Elizabeth one more time then escorted her to her family, calling for Miss Elizabeth's cloak.

Caroline stood dazed with astonishment. After a moment, she turned and headed for the stairs. As she ascended, she heard footsteps and looked to see Col. Fitzwilliam walking out of the drawing room. He stepped into the hall and saw her looking his way. His gaze met hers, and Caroline knew in an instant that he had seen Darcy and Elizabeth kiss. He knew that she had seen it too.

"Good night, Col. Fitzwilliam," she said.

"Good night, Miss Bingley," he replied, with a nod of his head. He then turned and headed to where the Bennets waited with Bingley and Darcy.

With her steps heavy and tired, Caroline climbed the stairs to her room where she found the solitude and privacy she desperately needed to admit her certain defeat.

# *CHAPTER SEVENTEEN*

Col. Fitzwilliam kept his eye on the arrivals as they sashayed through the doorway of the dance hall, preening and posing coquettishly. The London season was in full swing and that night's ball was sure to be a crush. His season was not a success; no young woman of wealth would take a second son so quickly, and he was not yet at the point where he had to consider the desperate, aging women that had smiled at him from behind their fans in the previous weeks.

He had arrived at the assembly room when the doors first opened, positioning himself in the line of sight of the doorway, prepared to wait. He had news to share, and he wanted to use it to his advantage to procure the specific, comfortable, future of his dreams.

The object of his attention arrived at ten minutes past the hour—an arrival timed precisely, he suspected. Along with the familiar faces of her sister and brother-in-law, Miss Bingley was accompanied by two other young women to whom he had not previously been introduced. His gaze followed the party as they threaded their way through the growing crowd to where they positioned themselves on the side of the room. As soon as he saw them stop, he made his way over to them.

Warm greetings were exchanged and, wasting no time, Col. Fitzwilliam said, "May I have the honor of your first and second dances tonight, Miss Bingley?"

"Why, yes, thank you," Caroline replied quickly. She introduced Col. Fitzwilliam to her friends, one Miss Abigail Wilson and one Miss Hazel Burke-Thomson, and as a gentleman would do, he applied to dance with both of them after his turns with Caroline.

Polite conversation ensued until the master of ceremonies called the first dance. Col. Fitzwilliam offered his hand, and Caroline let him lead her to the dance floor. The music began and they stepped into the dance.

Wasting no time, Col. Fitzwilliam said, "It is wonderful to see you. It feels like old times."

"It feels the same for me as well," Caroline replied.

"Sadly, I have news to relate that will make it impossible for those days to return," he said.

"Oh?" Caroline replied. He saw her tighten her expression in anticipation.

"It is the news we both foresaw. Darcy has become engaged to Miss Elizabeth Bennet. Of course, as soon as he put off coming to London to stay in a suite of rooms at the Meryton Arms, I knew this ending was inevitable."

He tightened his grip on her hands, fearing she might swoon.

But Caroline was made of tougher stuff, despite not being able to hide her disappointment completely.

"Thank you for telling me," she said stiffly. After a moment's pause, she said wearily, "So she has won," and shook her head. "Pemberley seems too big for her."

"Yes, I suppose it does," Col. Fitzwilliam agreed. "For what it is worth, I believe you would have done a fine job as its mistress."

"Thank you," she said.

"So fine that I have made some inquiries that I would like to discuss with you further."

"Whatever do you mean, Col. Fitzwilliam?" Caroline's dour expression perked up.

"While I cannot change Darcy's mind, I don't believe you must be exiled from his company."

"Who says I desire his company anymore?"

"My apologies. I understood that we both placed being in the company of Darcy and Pemberley above all others."

"Perhaps at one time," she protested.

"Very well," he decided to drop the subject. "May I still call on you tomorrow to discuss a pressing matter of great importance to your future?"

"Of course, Col. Fitzwilliam. As an old friend, you are always welcome."

They changed the subject to the weather and the present company. By the end of the second dance, Caroline felt as if the shock of the bad news was already wearing off.

She returned to the sidelines, both figuratively and literally, she thought to herself. Drawing close to Mrs. Hurst, she whispered into her ear, "It is done. Darcy and that Bennet tart are engaged. I am sure Bingley will ask Jane next, and the Bennets will have won everything—all the best men and houses, while I have nothing."

"Ah," Mrs. Hurst replied, studying her sister's face. "Then you must marry Col. Fitzwilliam instead, if you can. You must save face."

"What do you mean, save face?"

"The entire town of Meryton and the ton here in London know that you have practically thrown yourself at Darcy for the past year. Unless you can add good news of your own, you can expect your reputation to feel the effect."

"My reputation?"

"Yes. I am sorry if I sound harsh," Mrs. Hurst whispered. "But in these types of situations, you must counter Darcy's news with good news of your own. You must marry Col. Fitzwilliam. Everyone knows he is interested in you but you were always Darcy or nothing."

"Everyone knows? But he hasn't asked," Caroline hissed back.

"Of course he hasn't asked. He is too intelligent to ask a question when he is certain that the answer will be no. I would have lost respect for him if he had asked you when Darcy was unattached. But Darcy is lost, and you must accept that and move on," Mrs. Hurst whispered fiercely.

"He is coming to call tomorrow," Caroline explained. "With some information he says is important to my future."

"Is he? That is a lucky break for you, my dear. We will make ourselves scarce tomorrow so he has the privacy he may require. And let us call it an early night here as well before word of Darcy's engagement gets out and the assembled start whispering and looking your way. Mr. Hurst! Mr. Hurst! We are leaving!"

"But what of Abigail and Hazel? We just arrived here, and Col. Fitzwilliam has promised them dances," Caroline grabbed onto her sister's sleeve as she made to move away.

"Tell them we have to depart but that Mr. Hurst will leave the carriage for them," she replied, her tone commanding.

"But how will we get home?"

"We will walk. The fresh air will tire you out so you may sleep well and look your best tomorrow morning for Col. Fitzwilliam. Now go quickly and meet me by the door as soon as you can." She turned her back on her sister and hurried away to collect her husband.

Caroline meant to object to her sister's pushy ways but was too surprised by her proclamation that she was on the brink of humiliation to think straight. She apologized to Abigail and asked her to relay the news of their unexpected departure to Col. Fitzwilliam and Hazel when they finished their dance. Caroline scurried back to the front door, where Mr. and Mrs. Hurst were standing with their cloaks. They handed over Caroline's cloak and walked out into the night.

"Keep up, will you?" Mr. Hurst scowled at Caroline. "For it is on your account that I am forced to walk, and I wish to get it over with as quickly as possible."

Caroline pushed herself a little harder, but her dance shoes were thin and delicate and the winter streets cold.

"There is no need for you to be so rude," she complained.

"You are no longer the future mistress of Pemberley, so I may now say whatever I like!" Mr. Hurst snapped back.

"Mr. Hurst!" Mrs. Hurst exclaimed. "Control yourself. Caroline simply took a risk and lost, something you, with your bad luck at cards, should understand."

"I've a right to my opinion, haven't I, especially when it involves my own comfort! And if you don't like my comments, I'll send you back to Netherfield first thing in the morning so I can have me some peace," he grumbled but he refrained from further rude remarks for the remainder of the walk home.

Caroline fumed inwardly at Mr. Hurst's remarks.

How dare he throw her disappointment in her face and threaten her with Netherfield!

She had a mind to start a fire in his own kitchen but since Col. Fitzwilliam was coming the next day, she thought better of it.

The walk home required less than ten minutes of exertion, and upon entering the residence, they all separated and wordlessly went to their rooms. Caroline slammed the door to her room firmly, knowing that the sound would reverberate and rattle Mr. Hurst but she did not care.

Darcy to marry Elizabeth!

She felt as if she knew him not. She felt as if she had no insight at all regarding any man. They would do what they liked, even if it were the opposite of what they said they would do the day before.

Would Col. Fitzwilliam even show up tomorrow? He was a man, after all, prone to inconstancy like all his gender, so that meant he might not.

But there was something in his manner that made her think a proposal was forthcoming. She knew she did not love Col. Fitzwilliam; she loved Darcy. Or thought she had. But she and Col. Fitzwilliam did share a friendship that she thought might be enough of a start. She vowed to consider whatever offer he brought. Otherwise, she feared that her return to Netherfield was imminent.

***

Caroline was seated in the drawing room the next morning, waiting somewhat anxiously for her caller, when she heard the knocker rap on the door. She stood up, smiled serenely, and held the expression as Col. Fitzwilliam entered the room.

In his hands were a large bouquet of cut flowers and a rolled-up set of papers; the appearance of which was quite intriguing.

"Good morning, Miss Bingley," Col. Fitzwilliam began with a proper bow, handing her the flowers.

She nodded, took the bouquet and returned his greeting. "Won't you sit down?"

He obliged. She put down the flowers and seated herself across from him. "My sister and her husband are out and send their regrets at having to miss you."

"Thank you. It is advantageous for us, though, don't you think, to have privacy?"

Caroline smiled in agreement and started to say how much she enjoyed the company when they were all together, but he cut her off.

"Miss Bingley, I must speak frankly to you. I am here to offer you my hand in marriage. I apologize for being transactional in the offer that I am about to make to you, but you are a woman who I believe appreciates frankness and honesty. Since we first met, I have admired you for your discipline and dedication to a cause, even if that cause was securing my cousin's affections and his home. I have long known that you would not take me while there was still a chance to win Darcy, but now that he is betrothed to another, I will be bold and tell you that I am here for you, if you will have me. I am not rich like Darcy, but, if you pardon my directness, your brother has assured me that you have an income that is plenty for the both of us."

"That is true. It has never been a secret," she replied.

"By accepting my offer, you will gain a loyal and committed spouse who holds much affection and admiration for your person. And as I remain Darcy's closest cousin and most trusted confidante, in marrying me you will become a permanent member of Pemberley's inner circle. So, while I am not Fitzwilliam Darcy, might you consider a life with me to be the next best thing?"

All the while he was speaking, Caroline's face blushed a deeper and deeper shade of red in a mixture of astonishment and embarrassment to see her aims and motives so boldly described.

"Col. Fitzwilliam! This is quite a surprising soliloquy you have made. I …"

"Please, there is more for you to consider." Col. Fitzwilliam stood up, took the rolled-up papers, untied the ribbon that kept them in place and unfurled them on the top of the pianoforte. He invited Caroline to come closer.

Caroline's gaze took in the papers and gasped. Before her were the renderings of Chipperton, the Derbyshire manse that Bingley stubbornly refused to let for her. How she would never have heard the name Netherfield Hall if he had only listened to her back then!

"Chipperton?" she asked.

"Then you remember it?"

She nodded yes.

"I have made serious inquiries, and it is still available. I recently corresponded with our family architect, who has offered significant suggestions for its improvement should we be happy there and decide to purchase. My father has agreed to gift me sufficient money to make it into my own, I mean, our own home, should you accept my proposal. Please, my dear friend. What do you say?"

She looked up from the renderings. He stood there silently, gazing at her with such earnestness that Caroline's stubborn pride finally melted away and was replaced by a feeling akin to triumph.

She would be a Darcy, after all!

Or close enough.

And Chipperton! How she loved the place! Why, she would fix it up so grandly that it would be talked about by all the neighbors. And when she got bored with her days, they'd take the carriage over to Pemberley and be treated like family. Col. Fitzwilliam's offer was everything her rejected heart longed for, but it was more than that.

She would have her own life. And her own home.

She would never have to return to Netherfield.

There was no value in being coy at such a moment.

"Yes," she said automatically.

He took her hand.

"Then you will do me the greatest honor of becoming my wife?"

"Thank you, Col. Fitzwilliam. It is a very thoughtful proposal. I accept."

"Are you certain?"

"Yes," she nodded. "We will make a good team. You may kiss me."

Somewhat surprised to have been so readily accepted, Col. Fitzwilliam leaned in and kissed his betrothed. Having both secured what they desired for their future, they found themselves to be quite content.

For the next hour, they sat in familiar companionship and discussed their future life at Chipperton. Col. Fitzwilliam explained the modernizations he had in mind and what rooms they would take for their own suites. The time passed pleasantly, until, unable to contain their curiosity, Mr. and Mrs. Hurst burst in the door.

Caroline stood up quickly and said, "Congratulate us. We are engaged."

"How wonderful! May I extend my most heartfelt

congratulations" Mrs. Hurst exclaimed, and Mr. Hurst pumped Col. Fitzwilliam's hand and added his hearty congratulations. Col. Fitzwilliam was promptly invited to stay for luncheon, and the misery of the past few months was exchanged for a joyous day full of hope for the future.

After a leisurely luncheon, Col. Fitzwilliam begged their forgiveness and took his leave, and Mr. Hurst left to spend the afternoon at his club. The day was clement, the sun was out in a cloudless sky, and Mrs. Hurst and Caroline desired to promenade in the park. They decided to call on Miss Hazel and Miss Abigail to tell them the good news and invite them to promenade with them.

On the way there, Mrs. Hurst said, "Well done. So you gained a life in Derbyshire after all."

"Yes, and avoided social humiliation at the same time," Caroline replied with relief.

"To be honest, I find Col. Fitzwilliam to be the better match for you, as he does not withdraw in society as Mr. Darcy does," Mrs. Hurst confessed.

"Honestly, my head was so turned by Pemberley that I couldn't see how right Col. Fitzwilliam was for me. I have always been so comfortable with him, and he in return has accepted me and approved of me readily. It is quite a refreshing feeling after all that striving after Darcy."

"So, a happy ending," Mrs. Hurst declared.

"Yes, today I am quite happy. And now that I am to live in Derbyshire, no one can ever force me to go back to Netherfield Hall, which has been the source of much misery for me," Caroline decreed.

"Not even for the wedding I fear will now happen between Bingley and Jane?"

"I may make one exception, but only the one."

After collecting Miss Hazel and Miss Abigail, the foursome set out to promenade in the nearby park. Caroline's friends were delighted to hear of her news, albeit slightly disappointed that the very gallant Col. Fitzwilliam was off the market so quickly after making his acquaintance.

"Do not despair, for you never know when the right match will come into your life," Caroline said, feeling content enough in her good fortune to be encouraging.

"You may even have your eye set on another suitor when the right one comes along," Mrs. Hurst added. "Besides, London is full of eligible men; use your season wisely."

They continued to promenade, discussing the previous night's assembly and Caroline's wedding clothes when Mrs. Hurst suddenly stopped still in her path and clutched Caroline's arm.

"Oh, dear. Oh no," she whispered. "How dreadfully awkward."

Alarmed, Caroline said, "What is it? What is wrong?"

"Do not look straight ahead, fix your gaze elsewhere, but if I am not mistaken, Mr. Waxman is heading straight for us."

"Mr. Waxman from Bath?" Caroline's heart stopped at the memory. "Is my luck that horrid that I should run into him on this the happiest of days?"

"It appears so."

Mr. Waxman spotted his two old acquaintances and, waving his cane at them, came rushing forward.

"Mrs. Hurst, Miss Bingley. What a surprise!"

"How do you do? What a surprise to run into you," Caroline said, offering only a half-smile in return.

"Yes, I am just arrived in London for what I hope to be a very profitable season," he said, eyeing Caroline greedily. His signature scent of old tobacco hung around him. Caroline so wished that she could cover her nose with her handkerchief.

"Allow me to introduce my two friends, Miss Wilson and Miss Burke-Thomson," Caroline replied coolly.

The two friends nodded their greeting. Mr. Waxman smiled with marked disinterest and then quickly turned his overbearing attention back to Caroline.

"Will I see you at the next ball? How about tonight's concerto? Have you tickets? I've managed to procure tickets."

Mrs. Hurst exclaimed, "Mr. Waxman, you are more than generous, but I am afraid we must decline, albeit for very happy reasons. As you have just arrived in town then you will not have heard the news. Miss Bingley is engaged to Col. Fitzwilliam. It is just being announced. He is the cousin and trusted advisor of Fitzwilliam Darcy of Pemberley—you must know how very grand a place that is. Miss Bingley and the colonel are planning to take up residence in an adjacent property where they will all be very happy."

His disappointment was clearly visible, but he managed to congratulate Caroline and wish her the best.

He turned his gaze to Miss Abigail and Miss Hazel and said, "I have two tickets for tonight's concerto. Please join me."

"I am afraid that is impossible," Mrs. Hurst intervened. "For they leave tonight on the six o'clock to York. Terribly bad timing."

"Oh, that is too bad," he mumbled, and then staring off over Caroline's shoulder, he recognized another society matron whose favor he wished to incur, and he bowed suddenly and took his leave.

The group was silent for a few more paces. Finally, Miss Wilson said, "Thank you for providing an excuse for us. How did you come to know him? He is so unlike Col. Fitzwilliam!"

"Mr. Waxman was a very pushy man whom Miss Bingley had the misfortune to attract in Bath. We had to leave town to be rid of him."

"He smelled odd," observed Miss Burke-Thomson. "I dare say I could not have endured an entire concerto in his vicinity."

"I do believe that half the difficulty of being in society is extricating one's self from the company of undesirables," Mrs. Hurst said.

"Sometimes by drastic measures," Caroline added, smiling at her sister, who laughed with her but could never fully know the lengths to which Caroline had gone to in that regard. Caroline continued, "But the important thing to remember is that you should always be ready to pack your bags and make a hasty exit should your circumstances require you to do so."

The two young women nodded in acknowledgement of their companions' wisdom.

"How unfortunate to run into Mr. Waxman!" Caroline exclaimed. "I hope and pray he knows no one in Derbyshire and that my future husband and I may walk the streets in my new hometown without fear of meeting him." She felt a warm glow of delight in proclaiming Derbyshire her future home and, she realized, an equal degree of pride and affection in calling Col. Fitzwilliam her future husband.

***

Caroline and Col. Fitzwilliam were married four months later and a week before Elizabeth and Darcy and Jane and Bingley held their joint ceremony.

After leasing Chipperton for a short period of time, the newlyweds were so delighted in it that they made it their own. Caroline fitted it up with new furniture and draperies, all made to her exacting and expensive standards.

Col. Fitzwilliam insisted that the kitchen be modernized like Netherfield. He also insisted that all care was to be taken by the staff to double check that the doors were locked each night, as he had once been forced to rescue his wife from a kitchen fire set by a vagabond that had somehow entered by stealth. The young maids all found the idea of being rescued in the middle of the night by one's future husband to be very romantic.

Privately, Caroline reprimanded her husband for repeating the story too many times, emphasizing that his unchaperoned entry into her room reflected badly on him and brought up feelings of embarrassment on her end that she found difficult to overcome. He promised never to mention it again, which pleased Caroline very much. She was no longer that desperate young woman who had set Netherfield Hall on fire and she had no desire to be constantly reminded of her past mistakes.

The new couple called regularly at Pemberley. Despite their initial differences, Caroline came to admire Mrs. Elizabeth Darcy. She found her to be a woman possessing rare common sense and a biting wit. Caroline often found herself laughing out loud at Mrs. Darcy's pointed observations, and before long, considered her one of her closest friends. However, to Caroline's great surprise, she noted how Elizabeth made no significant changes to the rooms of Pemberley, letting the décor exist in the taste and style of a previous generation.

What a waste, Caroline thought.

Life in Derbyshire was so pleasant that even the new Mr. and Mrs. Bingley were drawn to it. Bingley decided to forego renewing his lease at Netherfield to move closer to Darcy and Elizabeth. He and Jane found a charming home older than Pemberley and made it their own. Caroline thought it all a little sad and shabby, lacking in any kind of modern elegance and housing too many pets. But her brother always would be fond of old dogs and sofas and who was she to try and change him? Besides, Bingley was Jane's problem now.

## *Also by Olivia Kane*

Elizabeth Bennet's Wedding

A Very Meryton Christmas

The Five Graces of Longbourn

Trouble with the Earl

Trouble with Wickham

Printed in Great Britain
by Amazon

67584614R00125